Winner of the 2012

Kenneth Patchen Award

For Innovative Fiction

How to Break Article Noun

by Carolyn Chun

Journal of Experimental Fiction 46

JEF Books/Depth Charge Publishing
Geneva, Illinois

Kenneth Patchen Award widget
designed by Michael J. Seidlinger
Cover Art by Deborah Chun

ISBN 1-884097-12-X

ISBN-13 978-1-884097-12-6

ISSN 1084-847X

The foremost in innovative fiction
http://experimentalfiction.com

How to Break Article Noun

by Carolyn Chun

Contents

2

Carolyn Chun

Acknowledgments

The author gratefully thanks Mom, Laura, June, Jeff, and Tim for their readings of and feedback on this manuscript. She thanks them together with Dad, Deb, Tom, Steve, and Mike for invaluable personal support. Without these individuals, this novella would not be possible. A large debt is also owed to the inspirations of Scripture, Claude Monet, Claude Debussy, Marguerrite Duras, Italo Calvino, Stephen Hawking, Mareike, Troy, Evan, and countless others, for the completion of this piece.

How to Break Article Noun

Abstract

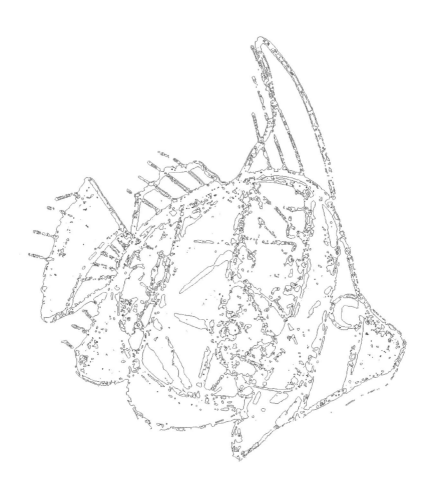

Carolyn Chun

Introduction.

I didn't want to have a love story until I found life to be
an abiding romance with the world. I didn't want to write a love
story until I found life to be an abiding romance with words.

***

I: Entropy

1. "Was it another simile?"

      "Can you close the door and sit down? Something bad," he says, meaning *I have something bad to tell you.* Her bedroom door soft and light shut smooth as the wing of a swan. His eyes fixed on the bed like that are full of dark portents.

2. how they met underwater: a five-part composition in which their names are assigned

one

Don't expect her to say what she means. "I miss you," means something's wrong. "Everything's wrong," means she misses you. It's unclear whether or not she knows this herself.

He would do anything for her and holds this against her.

She finds honesty unbecoming. Honesty is the language of desperation.

He is a literalist. He is aware of and frustrated by her indifference to literalism, though enchanted by her language.

She somehow matches the tone of her voice to the shade of her eyes.

He pulls the door shut behind him, wonders where he is.

It is unclear whether or not she ever means anything. This delights and puzzles her. She is so delightful that she may be forgiven anything. (Her mother tells her so.)

When he pulls the door shut behind him, the sound of it

surprises him. He feels bewildered. It's night now; the moon looms. He glides through weeds. Her backyard is a jungle. He opens the squeaky fence gate and passes through. Now he feels nothing. His eyes neither blink nor see for a full few seconds. It's amazing. He is empty of his own presence. His presence returns precisely upon noticing this fact, and he unlocks his car door.

A realization slightly shocks her features. She stares at a purple and yellow fish made from pieces of broken glass, volcanic glass, she thinks, and a red garnet eye. It's on her mantle, sharp and light over the dull, pale bricks. Fish scales from volcanic fires. The urge surfaces suddenly, from an unknown place: she'd like to break it. She'd like to throw it down against the bricks. Then lift shards and fling them down again. She won't do it, though. She'd never do a thing like that. (She considers her restraint a fault.)

The moonlight in the driveway opens the night, proves its emptiness to him. Behind his car is a box of recyclables: empty spaghetti sauce jars, cereal boxes, glass juice bottles. Inside the box, the lighting is dim. He can't make out the colors on the labels. Maybe they are black and white. It would be appropriate.

She considers breaking a glass bottle. Something from the recycling bin, something that she can wrap her hand around. Cool to the touch. And weighted properly. With a smooth neck.

Carolyn Chun

Behind the driveway is an open field, a grass yard, white in the moonlight. And then a white picket fence points up toward the midnight sky, the setting moon. Between the fence and the sky a city on the horizon. A world.

She imagines the fish breaking. It might happen like this: As the movers set down the red sofa, maybe one of the four legs pushes a wasp that has flown in the propped-open door. The wasp leaps spitefully into the air, throwing herself at the larger of the two deliverers. He swings both arms. Perhaps she grabs a book and shoos the bug out the door, but not before the windmilling man has upset the glass fish resting on the mantle. It sits back deeply before leaning sharply forward, and then erupts on the brick stoop of the fireplace with a stunning, chiming chord. The man's mouth opens in surprise while his brow furrows deeply in disbelief. She, surprised by how calm she feels, kneels over the wreck, touches the bent metal, the shards of volcanic glass. The man utters something or other. She lifts the thin, metal frame of the ruined fish, and turns it over. It seems heavier in her hand than ever before. She drops it down again, on its back this time, against the brick stoop where it bounces and is still, reduced to a few shards of glass clinging to a metal frame like sharp teeth in a mouth. The movers are silent and embarrassed.

He can only rest when he has something to do. If he has nothing to do, he is restless. He has trouble sleeping. As soon as he's given a task, he can fall asleep. When he has nothing to do, he dissolves into the task of doing nothing. When he does

9

nothing, he is nothing. He doesn't want to get into his car. He doesn't know where to go.

She considers wrapping it in a towel, fingering the thin ribs of iron between the papery glass shards. She places a hand on the soft towel, presses down against the fish, feels its form rise up against her palm. Next, she rubs the back of this hand with her other hand, and shoves down like she's doing CPR. The fish exhales.

He knows that she is the softest thing he'll ever touch. She has told him so. What does it mean? She's gone now, but it stays with him, the softness. He is surprised by the gentle suppleness of it. And it is unyielding sometimes. So that he feels a pressure when he breathes: a heaviness first in the air, then in his lungs. It's night. The moon has already set. He finds that he is pulling on his earlobe, his head tilted, his gaze has drifted down and off to the side.

> *I suffocate in an empty room.*
> *You know I am simple and ordinary.*
> *Gleaming fish swim through my thoughts.*

He recalls a poem she wrote for him. The first time she read it to him, her voice swung like a hammock. He looks around, wonders for a moment what he's doing outside, then remembers. It's dark. The moon has set or else not risen yet.

Carolyn Chun

I may surface in the crest of a nighttime swell.
I may cough up on a white beach.

He thinks she may have been describing the beach they drove past once. He recalls it now. The rain had just finished. The sky was blue-gray, the clouds clammy and close. They drove between autumn oak trees, glistening red and orange leaves. And then a long break in the trees on their right, and she'd looked up from the reclined passenger seat of his car to see a sandy stretch of beach along a still pool of empty water. He remembers the beads of water zigging down the window, a distant peal of thunder, the smell of fog.

I am nothing. I am exactly this:
moved by water, attended by sunlight.

He thinks about these words as he turns his keys over in his hand. The keys are hard and sharp. He'd like to break something. He scratches his neck with his car key.

Inside, every light is on. She has lain down on the red sofa. If you wanted to, you could believe that she is asleep. She is on her side with her hands folded under her neck. She is not sure if he will come back inside. She has been here for quite some time. If he comes back, she will wake up. She is tired and wants him to come inside now.

How to Break Article Noun

It might rain. Dark clouds block out the stars. He is in a box now: between a gate and a white fence, between asphalt and dark clouds (cold drops of water), between a girl and a drive, the past and the uncertain present. He feels as if no sound would emerge if he spoke right now. Or, even if he heard it, nobody else would.

She might break the fish in the bathtub. That would be appropriate. She looks down at it, still below the settling surface of the water, the edge of the white tub cold against her arms, the tiled floor icy beneath her bare feet as she crouches. She is unsure how to progress now, how the glass will break underwater, what it will sound like.

He thinks it might rain. It would be appropriate now, for his skin to be coated with water. It would help to describe the glass box he feels around him, the distance between himself and every soft thing. His senses are zipped up. He doesn't know where he wants to go now. Something is filling the air. Quiet. Is he crying here, in the dark? He doesn't know.

She stretches and turns over. She wonders if she has locked the door. (She has.) She is wrapped in a soft, white blanket. It mimics a cloud. She feels soft. Like a cloud passing through mist. She stops waiting for him and goes to sleep.

He taps the car key along the windshield. The precise *clink clink clink* fills his mind. He imagines dipping his fingers in cool water. It's dark. The moon has set or not yet risen.

She's tired now. She feels exceptionally heavy. On the couch, with her back to him, she doesn't think she could raise her eyelids or voice. She has aged almost perceptibly since he left: her skin feels dry and fragile.

His back is to her now. His face feels cold. Is he crying here in the dark? He has aged almost perceptibly since being in the house: his eyes darken, he has trouble focusing.

That sharp-finned fish. She'd like to snap it like the hollow wing of a bird. Like a thin wrist. Because it is so impossibly fragile, so luminous and exquisite. Because it must be broken. Because of the shards it contains; the fragments that will dazzle out.

He turns the key in the lock, opens the car door, and sits down behind the steering wheel. When he shuts the door, he is in a glass bowl.

two

Inside the soft folds of blanket, Noelle is asleep. She dreams the earlier conversation with Isaac.

"Underneath is what the up there was," Isaac begins,

stepping through the door. The door reappears before him. He turns the key in the lock, opens the door, strides into the foyer. He loosens the dark tie around his neck; he's dressed handsomely in a white shirt and gray suit pants. His necktie is swimming with fish of various, deep colors. They wiggle up and downstream, disappearing into his collar at the top, and flipping smoothly at the dam bordering the bottom of the tie.

"Underneath is what the up there was," Isaac says, for the first time. "Haven't you been to the old perjury board? I hate to steal, lie, cheat, gamble, defame. But I seem to know, now, pretty dear."

Noelle looks up from her bowl of Wheat-O's at the sound of his voice. She listens to ten quick strides, and then his face swings in the doorway. They smile when their eyes meet. The crunching of the cereal is loud in her ears, but he may have said something about what was, or something up there, or maybe he has told her she is pretty.

"Did you meet anyone interesting today?" Noelle asks between munches. "Or go someplace interesting? How's your back?"

"Below my feet is the sky. I trod on the black blank between stars. I can't see lightning because I am lightning, or was. Noelle, my pretty dear, what are you taking of mine?" Isaac asks as he takes a seat across the table from Noelle. He talks like this in her dreams because her understanding of their earlier conversation is vague.

The dining room is on the west side of the townhouse,

and the window catches the lingering lavender flutters of the departed sun remembered by low clouds. The room is an airy, yellow print, and the furniture is all darkly stained wood. The overhead chandelier contains fifty lit candles, in whose light the darkening room is beginning to swim. Each shadow is cast in several directions behind Isaac and Noelle, but their faces are clear to each other. The room is bare except for the chairs and the table with its spread: a Wheat-O's box, a gallon milk container, a bowl of cereal. The crunching of cereal is the only sound in the place.

"The sky *is* amazing this evening," Noelle agrees, turning toward the window. She experiences the symptoms of miscommunication without placing their cause. The fish on his tie have metal skeletons and glass eyes. Isaac pulls a yellow and purple one off of his tie and drops it on the table, where the fish convulses. Noelle would like to return the fish; she is beginning to feel just awful. "Yes, let's go out and see the stars tonight. Though there are enough clouds to wonder about rain. But what do we have to lose? An evening? Besides, we have others."

Noelle would enjoy an evening in the rain with him. He would not enjoy it, though; it would be lost to him. (She knows this even in her dream. Correction: she knows this better in her dream.) He realizes exactly how many of his evenings are in this woman's possession. They are twenty-six and twenty-seven. He computes it as a percentage and feels betrayed.

"I realize how many evenings were mine that are in a woman's possession! I am inside what has up the down. And around these two-by-fours, what have I here to know my own darkness? Your piercing eyes undo my uncertain probabilities. You blink between collapsing the wave functions of my life and death. What am I except the thing you see, the one drawn to your view?"

Isaac does not expect Noelle to understand Schrödinger's equations or Heisenberg's uncertainty principle. He doesn't completely understand them himself, except that Noelle makes things about him certain, she fixes him steadfast in her gaze. The townhouse is hers, and he is hers, because he has settled into the pool of her company, the glass bowl of her vicinity. The crinkly munching of cereal is loud in his ears; for a full moment, he forgets which of them is eating.

"You want to go down to the basement to fix the rotten two-by-fours? It's dark there; the bulb is still out. I'll replace it tomorrow maybe. Probably. I'm about ready to collapse, too. Did you drive anywhere nice? Did you like the view?"

Noelle is tired from the gym, and is in fact still in her gym clothes. She works out every Saturday, while Isaac chauffeurs wealthy businessmen to and from airports and various other destinations. Today the luxury sedan he drives passed 100,000 miles, and continued climbing. Noelle works at a local elementary school on weekdays. They have been like this for years. She would maybe like to get married.

"Within the ever-so-far-reaching palms of your hands are the contents of my life. And what are they?" Isaac picks up the box of cereal and swings his arm out over the floor; the box dangles between his thumb and middle finger. "The margin's all used up here. The space is expired, extinguished, exhaled. It must be yours, pretty dear. I'm so sorry to leave now." He drops the box, which lands on the floor open and upright, without spilling a single bite. "I must leave to have uncertainty—to not know again."

"Sweetheart," Noelle says over the low, empty sound of Isaac pushing his chair back. It sounds empty because the floor is hollow. "Sweetheart, you seem all in a rush. You have left my box on the floor." Noelle gobbles another bite of cereal, and looks up at Isaac, standing in the doorway. "Isaac, were you just describing your drive out to the edge of town?" Noelle knows something has happened while she has been chewing her cereal. Isaac looks sad. "Do you feel sick?"

Isaac looks sad because he feels as though the air is full of Noelle, and he cannot remember what else the air is like. He compares himself to a kite, and Noelle to a breeze. He wants to feel that he may be still and uncertain, and unmoved, again. This is unappealing and necessary, he has decided. He doesn't know what it means to float on the air. He's not sure who he is if he is not his own. Yes, she does ascribe these values to Isaac in her dreams, in her grief. The man of her dreams is unavailable. The unavailable is the man of her dreams.

The evening is over. The spoon is in the bowl. They have each left the room. She lies on the couch facing a mantle that holds a bright fish made of pieces of broken glass. He approaches the door to the backyard. When she dreams that she falls asleep later, she dreams she dreams the earlier conversation with Isaac.

"Underneath is what the up there was." Isaac is swimming toward her. She looks up from her cereal at him. He is outside the dining room window, blowing bubbles at her that rise up toward the darkening sky, and the lavender tufts of clouds. The flames of the chandelier candles swim over her head. The sky looks like rain.

three

The following conversation between the boy and the girl precipitated the opening and closing of the back door of her apartment in close concert with the exit of the boy. Sitting in his car outside her house on the night he leaves, the boy recalls it, after he scratches his neck with his key. The entire recollection spans the length of one blink of his eyes.

"Are you awake then?" he asks the white blanketed lump stirring on the couch. As he asks, his eyes never leave the page of the paperback he is reading in the nearby rocking chair.

The blanket kicks its feet in response.

"Noelle, here's a story about us: in a pine tree forest filled with yellow sunlight, a couple is walking. There's some fresh snow crunching underfoot, under their boots, that is. And they are wearing scarves wrapped around their faces. They don't ever say a word to one another. Every so often they turn toward each other or look in the same direction, and they share these

18

moments instead of conversation. And it's like us except you've got a blanket on instead of a scarf."

As she sits up, her face emerges from the blanket. She experiences a flicker of confusion and is surprised by his face. There is a glass fish over there on the mantle.

"Am I the snow crunching or am I the boot?" she asks with a wide yawn.

"Hmm?"

"Am I the words they don't say or am I the looks in the same direction? This is a story about me and you, I?" she asks, shortening Isaac's name.

"Yes, No," he says, shortening Noelle's name. "You and I are like the people walking through the woods. That's all I mean."

"So I'm the pine tree forest and you're the yellow sunlight, then, because I'm under a white blanket and you, sir, are warm and bright. I am full of wind. You gently lean into dark places. You commune with the birds of the air and the fish of the sea. I am trapped, I guess. Under a frozen blanket. Have I got it right?"

"Sure. I guess so." Isaac feels nervous. He experiences the symptoms of miscommunication without naming their root. Yes, he does ascribe these games to Noelle in his recollection. The girl in the blanket is bored; he is beginning to feel just awful.

"I had a dream while I slept beneath this frozen blanket. It was also about us."

For the first time in this conversation, he sets down his

19

book to look at her. "Was it another metaphor?"

"It wasn't a metaphor, it was déjà vu," she begins, her eyes studying the dull fish on the mantle. "In my dream, we were sitting here, exactly as we are now, except that we had to speak through some kind of invisible ether. As I spoke, you watched my mouth form words, but the time delay between my speaking and your hearing expanded as I spoke. And, when you replied, the same problem. We interrupted each other several times, simply because of this, before we were no longer speaking, but instead, we turned toward each other every so often. And, every so often, we looked in the same direction.

"In my—" she continues.

"What do—" he interrupts.

"But, go ahead."

"No, after you."

"In my dream, I was a time delay, and you were a word."

"What do you mean?"

"Am I awake or asleep right now? Are you? We seem comfortable. Are we comfortable?"

"I'm comfortable. If you're comfortable, then we both are."

"Is it being comfortable that makes you not understand me? Not pay attention?" Isaac is not sure if this final pair of questions was voiced or implied and understood silently.

four

Neither the man in the car nor the woman asleep in the townhouse considers the possibility that this may have happened instead.

We will suppose Noelle to be wrapped in a blanket that resembles a white cloud, though we will imagine the interior of the cloud to be warm, not filled with ice crystals like clouds one might observe in the sky. Let her sit reclined on a red couch in the soft dark of a reading light just turned off over her head. Now Noelle is asleep. This is how she sleeps. Her head is tilted toward her shoulder, her chin is out, and her mouth slices open.

Isaac steals a sidelong glance at her. She is curled up on most of the couch and he is seated on the remainder. This is the year they will both be 27, though he will be 26 for the rest of this month. As he looks at her, he has the intense sensation of moving forward. It feels like a shove, but he has not just been jostled by her feet. Nor has he shifted in the slightest. It has to do with Noelle, with the hundred strands of brown hair that burst from the hair clip that comes open as she leans against it. The strands swivel out of place to slide along a smooth cheek and neck as he observes.

Isaac turns back to his book, *Man on a Couch*, propped on his crossed legs, but he's not reading the words. He's trying to place this feeling, this urgency. It seems familiar.

Later, her shoulders jerk slightly, and she wakes. He perceives these two facts. Noelle slides the window shade open to

Ursa Minor. Noticing the good view, she makes the following offer. "If I lean back, you'll have an easy angle on the constellation," she remarks as she touches his shoulder and tilts back in her seat.

Isaac has developed an appreciation for stars during the past year plus with her. "I'll just lean toward the window," he replies, pressing her down momentarily to look past her shoulder. It is a good view.

"Your response feels heavy to me," Noelle smiles, trying half-heartedly to push the gazing man off of her. "You know, I," she continues, shortening Isaac's name, "I think that you prefer leaning on me to being leaned on, which strikes me as a strange kind of pressure for me to feel. I confess that somehow I would like to be lifted, buoyed up by you. I don't know if that's immoral. I don't want to be on a pedestal. Also, this desire to be lifted up seems somewhat improper because I would also like to enjoy you instead of thinking about you too much."

She wonders aloud how long she was out. Noelle realizes that her thoughts have turned as a way of changing the subject. "I'm embarrassed by how much I've said," she admits, "and self-conscious of my embarrassment, to boot." She says it as a way of finding out if it's true. While she cares nothing for honesty, she appreciates truth.

He considers her self-conscious ramblings. "No," he begins, shortening Noelle's name, "let me push up a sleeve of my sweater to look at my watch." She has been out about half an hour, give or take. But she's no longer interested. "I wonder at your hasty comments and questions in addition to the jerk of your shoulders that woke you. They all seem connected: impulsive and, I can understand, embarrassing. You are strange this evening."

"Oh. Thanks. What are you reading?"

"Words. How was your nap?"

She doesn't remember how her nap was. "I'm glad that you are responding lightly again."

He imagines making conversation. *I'm Isaac. Nice to meet you.* Would she like that?

I'm Noelle. Put 'er there. She thinks as she imagines responding to the white, numinous folds of Isaac's small talk.

"Our conversation is beginning to feel to both of us like a *tête-à-tête*," Isaac says. "I used to enjoy the way this conversation would wake me up, though I was always slightly annoyed by the interruption of my thoughts and reading. It was new, once. This conversation, that is."

"I feel a burden to make conversation if there is to be any," Noelle replies. "Shall we return to our first conversation?" *Shall I ask you what you do? Shall you reply that you butcher fish and can slice and dice any living creature?*

"Shall I bring my hand up to touch my own neck? Shall I look in the mirror and imagine ways of cooking myself?" Isaac asks.

"Occupational hazard, I guess."

How old is this? Isaac wonders. "I was once glad to push the social envelope into uncertain territory. I used to really enjoy this conversation. When I first met you, I wanted to win at this somehow. The more you impressed me, the more I want to take you down. Or pin you down. I confess I want to dominate you. I feel both attracted and agitated. Maybe it's gone on too long. I don't know that I want this anymore."

"How old am I? I'm twenty-seven. Three cubed. This is the best year of my life."

"This year feels the same as last year to me, and the same as the one before that. Why do you say the best year of your life?"

Noelle doesn't know. She's always had a stiff upper lip, but she might cry. She lies now. "I know that it's the best year because it's happening right now. I enjoy the endless curiosity. So long as something will happen. Seriously, I, something is about to happen." She is crying now. How can he feel the same this year, when she loves him so much? Noelle thinks that she wants him to leave now.

"It's all happened before," Isaac lies. He is about to leave. He is about to open and close the door. They wonder how long they will wait, and how they will say it. They know it will happen tonight. Noelle feels like breaking something. Isaac feels like a fish in a glass bowl, or like the glass fish on the mantle over the fireplace. Each moment he circles the same territory, and he is no more than the collection of these moments. He is a collection of moments, an impoverished collection of circles. They both look at the mantle now, at the center of the mantle, at a fish made from pieces of broken glass. Noelle is the first to realize that they are both holding their breath.

five

We will suppose the girl to be wrapped in a blanket that resembles a white cloud, though we will imagine the interior of the cloud to be soft, not filled with lightning like clouds one might observe in the sky. Let her sit reclined on an airplane in the soft dark of a reading light just turned off over her head. Now she is asleep. This is how she sleeps.

He steals a sidelong glance at her. She is in the window seat and he is on the aisle, seats 25A and 25B. This is the year they are both 25, though they haven't yet met. As he looks at her, however, he has the intense sensation of moving forward. It feels like a shove, but his chair has not been kicked just now by a youngster. Nor has the plane accelerated in the slightest. It has to do with her, with the hundred strands of brown hair that burst from the hair clip that comes open as she leans against it. The strands swivel out of place to slide along a smooth cheek and neck as he observes from her right side.

He turns back to his book, *Girl on a Plane*, propped against his snack table, but he's not reading the words. He's trying to place this feeling, this urgency.

Later, her shoulders jerk slightly, and she wakes. He perceives these two facts. She slides the window shade open to Ursa Major. "Oh, look," she says, her voice balanced between sleepiness and animation. "Ursa Major. What a good view!" Leaning back in her chair, she affords him an easy angle on the constellation.

"Hmm…" he says, leaning toward the window. "So it is."

His response feels slow to her. She feels stuck in a low speed, which is a strange kind of pressure to feel. She would like to speak quickly and be answered quickly and directly. This desire gives her a sense of impropriety because she would also like to enjoy his conversation instead of noticing this about his conversation.

"How long was I out?" she asks too fast. Now she is embarrassed at how quickly she has spoken, and self-conscious of her embarrassment.

"Hmm…" he replies, pushing up a sleeve of his dark gray sweater to look at his watch. "Hmm… You were out about half an hour, give or take." He wonders at the hasty comments and questions in addition to the jerk of her shoulders that woke her. They all seem connected, impulsive, and vaguely embarrassing. Now he wonders if it is inappropriate in any way for him to know how long she has been asleep.

"Oh. Thanks. What are you reading?"

"Words. How was your nap?"

She is glad that he is catching up to speed. "I don't remember. What's your name?"

"I'm Isaac. Nice to meet you."

"I'm Noelle. Put 'er there," she responds, sticking a hand

out from the white, numinous folds. Their conversation is beginning to feel to both of them like a *tête-à-tête*.

He shakes her hand swiftly. He's enjoying the way this conversation is waking him up, though he's slightly annoyed by this interruption of his thoughts and reading.

She feels the burden of making the conversation if there is to be any. "What's up, Isaac? What is it you do these days?"

"I work as a fish butcher these days. It's strange. Now that I know how to slice up an animal, I can't look at an animal without imagining slicing it up into parts. You know. Like ribs and legs and wings and a neck." Isaac realizes that he's brought his hand up to touch his own neck.

"That's what you think when you look in the mirror? You imagine how to cook yourself?"

"Occupational hazard, I guess. What do you do, if not butchering, Noelle?"

"I teach high school physics right now."

"Teaching is one way to be the smartest one in the classroom, I reckon."

"I've always wanted to be smartest!"

"How old are you?" Isaac asks, implying that she is acting childishly. He is glad to push her into uncertain territory. He is really enjoying this conversation. She is holding her own. Isaac wants to win at this somehow. The more Noelle impresses him, the more he wants to take her down. Or pin her down. He would win a wrestling match, if that makes him feel better. In truth, it does. Isaac can't quite place this sensation. He wants to dominate something somehow. He feels both attracted and agitated. Maybe it's the long flight.

"I'm twenty-five. Five squared. This is the best year of my life."

"That's strange—I'm five squared, too. But this year feels the same as last year to me, and the same as the one before that. Why do you say the best year of your life?"

"I don't know yet. I can just feel it." Noelle is lying, now. She knows that it's the best year of her life because it's not over yet, and she enjoys life only insofar as it is an endless curiosity. So long as something will happen, Noelle is having a good time. Right now, she feels excited, like something is about to happen. "How can this year feel the same as last year? This year is still happening."

"It's all happened before. Nothing new crops up once you're past twenty-one," Isaac claims, though he can sense that something new is happening. He can feel it. He is awake and ready. He accidentally imagines Noelle in pieces on his carving table, her face intact and challenging.

Carolyn Chun

3. man on a couch: from his own mouth

Statement by Isaac

Every utterance is a cry. I am town and town crier. Crying out is base. Paltry. Crying out is even vulgar, yet all take part, in some guise, some manifestation. The streets echo with what I am, revealing that one single thing I understand to whomever you are. These black and white streets. This "Statement" is a cry in which I attempt to name the various scaffolds that dapple and sway the one single thing.

In short, I worship the sacred human blank. It is capable of worship, transport, visions, double visions, multifold variegated visions, ecstasy, ecumenical excommunication, distress, dismantling, desire, disease, destruction, misdirection, abomination, self-suppression, sociopathy, crisis, mutilation, and suicide, particularly when expressed as a dire *idée fixe* of fatal urgency. Perhaps the ass finds an angel in the mirror, but observe the angel discovering the mortal angel, the ass finding a rotting horse. All share this instinct, no matter how boring.

Like everything sacred, these human states are not symbolic mimicry, but the present, thrashing truth: live embers from the burning core of blank. These behaviors are, by convention, withheld, boxed, and treated. We annihilate convention in order to experience the truth of otherness. We experience the pinnacle of something, transport from something to something, ecstasy. Lab animals and conservatives get electrocuted; seers, conservative in their own way, get electrified. This single, variegated thing. This one blinding thing. We strain, reach, hover, then plunge into that live fire. We are compelled by only this need. We are driven to death by this need. So it is.

I disclaim the responsibility to care about political and social structures. Perhaps I exist, here and now, operated upon by these tides. Yet I require not a political state, but a sensitive mental state in which all social sediment sloughs away to reveal a trembling. Trembling humanism. Lit like the sea. Imbued with the inchoate light and the brilliant blank—not a newspaper but a diary, not a diary but a tremendous ache.

Nevertheless I desire that fullness that historical landscape achieves, a fullness felt only in dreams. The traditional methods of pursuit have no place in my life. I prefer a tabula rasa to doilies and napkin rings. The human blank contains the particular history. This pursuit, though doomed, is the key. You may desire History; I will not satisfy you. Our only joy is the experience of otherness, and is achieved by a pursuit only the noblest and most perverse can sustain. Let those that must, find something.

Art that matters little to the artist is doomed. Nothing can come of nothing. I am crying in this town that there is a climax in human experience. I am holding on to it, immortalizing it, frozen in time with it. My self-discovery in this moment possesses this climax. Every moment of self-reflection, self-expression, self-creation carries in its wallet the currency of climax.

I am set free from history—that emotionless abstraction.

Carolyn Chun

Art is the only altar for the sacred human blank and my only home. There is no other fulfillment.

4. pin her down

"Can you close the door and sit down? Something bad," he says. Her bedroom door soft and light shut smooth as the stroke of a fish. His eyes fixed on the bed like that are bright as the nearing storm.

5. She is the first to realize they are both holding their breath.

The Corruption of Isaac's Statement by Noelle

I am made weightless by the hospitality of art: it is my only suitable home, and it is an invitation to nowhere. Self-creation is the construction of one's life, of one's home. Some people dwell on earth in wigwams or trailer parks, some people live in their relationships to other people, some people live geographically, some people live in their mastery of a role; I have dwelt in my relationship to art. This home is fleeting, falling apart even now as I speak of it. There's no place to lie down. This sentence may break under its own tiny weight.

Art that matters to the artist is doomed. Recall the fable of the grasshopper and the ant. The grasshopper fiddled all summer while the ant gathered food. During the winter, the ant ate literal food while the grasshopper dined on melody and air. Like an orchid. Which creature is alive? The ant, the grasshopper, the orchid, or the author? The art dearest to me is or was created out of that maniacal need to (or equally impossible attempt to) answer that one question. Every moment of self-discovery is starvation of something else. Why are we so cruel with ourselves? Why does aggressive art compel me more and more to lie down in its large mouth (broken glass teeth)? Why do I let die, that is, kill off, that is, annihilate in myself and others that soft hunger for preservation? Some part of my life sustains my life. Some part of my life sustains my art. I am not what I was or

33

will become. I am a vacuum presently between these two voids. Self-expression necessitates self-reflection, which begets self-destruction. I die at my own hands, in my own arms, in my cold stare, in my glassy reflection. Each moment of life carries in its wallet razor blades. Stare deeply into a moment, its edge against your eye.

Nevertheless I welcome the fullness that annihilation yields; that fullness which we feel in sleep but fumble to recall. The traditional methods of achieving death have no place in my life. Drugs, trance, meditation, religion, music. God is annihilating me by creating me. I have tried to live in my relationship to art, but only in the larger context of my relationship with God can I lie down. No part of me is safe unless it is loved, and if it is loved, then it may be sacrificed. Let those that must, love.

I claim the responsibility to care about the personal. Perhaps there is more than one human being, more than just one human being groaning at the edge of a deep abyss, breathing into cold absence.

Like the distance between two relativistic reference frames, the distance between two people is the width of a mind. If the distance is ever less than the width of a mind, then the effect is achieved by quantum tunneling, and is not sustainable. The universal conservation of energy requires the refund of the borrowed energy. Particle antiparticle annihilation will often suffice. Participle antiparticiple: making unmaking. So it is.

In short, I desire sacrifice, creation, destruction,

annihilation, sanctification, preservation, mutilation, direction, misdirection, non-direction, justification, lack of justification, resurrection, and love, especially when expressed in the reflective surface of a pool of water. I won't refute finding a face in the clouds, but I prefer, in a way, finding the clouds in a face. You understand and share this instinct though you are very boring. Lie down for a moment because you are very boring. I lie down because I am very very boring.

Every utterance is a lie. Lying is deemed indecorous by many, but all take part, at some pitch and timbre. This "Statement" is a lie in which I attempt to name the various dapples and sways of the summer air as seen through my upstairs window.

6. Are you awake then? This may be how they met.

　　　She tiptoes from plank to plank of the Southside Railroad track. She carefully places a toe on the bolt head on the left side of each plank and leans forward. Her mind counts the steps against her wishes: she tries to look up at the sky to distract herself from this counting caught in her brain like a fishhook caught in her mouth. He leans out of the woods a few feet down the tracks to look at her. In order to avoid bumping his face with her shoulder, she will have to deviate from her path or he will have to lean back. She pauses to consider. His brightopen eyes blink as if dazed.

　　　"What are you?" he asks, leaving out the word *doing*.

　　　"I'm listening for the smallest sound possible. I wonder what it will feel like, this new sound that I will experience. Perhaps I have heard it a great many times before hidden in the shadows of larger, leaning over sounds (restaurant dishes rattling, mouths mouthing, drums drumming). Perhaps it will feel like a cloud passing through mist."

　　　"You must cover your ears for a minute or two or ten, and then open them to hear the smallest sound possible. It's like adjusting your eyes to the dark by closing them. Close your ears from the bright loudness of your voice beside me, and open them again in the dark of my absence."

Carolyn Chun

She, in the habit of taking good advice that is easy to take, covers her ears up immediately while his face disappears back into the thick woods. In fact, she closes her eyes for good measure. What's more, she draws in a deep breath and holds it. Just as she obtains the breath to hold inside the pink walls of her lungs, her ribs charge in against them, followed rightupon by the expresstrain, which forces the sentence of air right back out.

The face in the woods begins to whistle, the mind entertaining no thought of death, of the physical incapability of opening again her downturned eyes.

7. He pulls the door shut behind him, wonders where he is. These are the last words they will ever speak.

"Can you close the door and sit down? Something bad," he says. Her bedroom door soft and light shut smooth as the close of an eye. His eyes fixed on the bed like that brightly foreshadow nearing headlights.

***

II: Contact

1. This may have happened.

A wind chime produces the sound of a vibrating column of air. The width and length of the pipe determine the resonant frequency of the hollow it contains. The chime is the voice of a cavity, a voice of the movement of wind. The Darling looks past her hands on the steering wheel long enough to forget whose hands they are.

His Sweetiepie is not on her way home. Honeycakes is instead on her way to LT's house.

Pumpkin is the only one who calls him LT, short for an old occupation of his: lion tamer. LT's fright, flight, fight instincts insist that he lift a chair and snap a whip. He is acutely aware that mouths hide tooth-filled caves. In a lion's mouth, each fang curves back toward the stomach: there is only one direction to go. In a lion tamer's dreams, he may be wrapped in the inner dark of a lion's belly, the skin of the belly stretched tight around its contents. After he realizes he can't pull a chair between himself and the beast he's entered, nor extend his arm to snap the whip, he begins to notice that he can't breathe.

LT wakes up gasping out of this dream now and lifts his face out of Love's long hair. It's not hair at all; it's just the twisted green pillowcase. His Angel's not even here. Now there is a knocking at the door downstairs. LT throws back the twisted blankets and wipes the sweat off his face with the back of his sleeve.

I am knocking on Lee Thomas's door. It's dark: the outside lights are off and the moon has set or else not yet risen. Each first-floor window of LT's house is covered with security bars. The door also has security bars over it, not that I can see them in this light. Trees lean in on both sides of me. Overhead, a light comes on. Darkness containing a layer of armor containing a bright cavity. I shift the grocery bags from my left hand to my right and remember that I'm still wearing my hunter green Hagglewares apron. Will the door open to reveal the bottom of a chair? No, just LT and his sleepy smile. He's dressed in a khaki sweatshirt and red flannel pajama pants. He opens the bars and I step over the threshold.

"Awesome. Hello, trusty Hagglewares employee Noelle."

"Hey." I untie the apron with the nametag, unnaming myself. "We aim to please. At Hagglewares, your house is our house! Hmm… Not Pookie? Or Sweetheart? Or even Apple Fritter?"

"Would you like to hear how many times I can say Noelle in one breath?"

It occurs to me that my very instinct for names is a vacancy. I'm aloof: I hardly know my name! Wasn't my brother

Ardent just accusing me of that very thing years ago? LT disappears and reappears sitting at the end of the couch. I sit at the other end, facing him. We aren't touching at all. (How would minds touch?)

Hic

I   The class last night was interesting. Should I tell you about the class?

LT   Yes.

I   He was one of Ardent's favorite Pentecostal speakers. The lecturer introduced the structure the class will have. He even mentioned one of my favorite verses, and taught us a new word: antinumianism.

LT   Antinumianism?

I   I think so. Can you pass me your dictionary? I don't want to get up. I'm perfectly comfortable.

LT   Here you go.

I   Thanks... Hmm. It's not in here. Antinumianism. It means "no law" or something. Something about the belief that grace excuses you from law.

LT   No laws of thermodynamics. No laws of physics. Hmm... Antinomianism?

I   Ah, yes. Antinomianism. It's right here. How did you know?

LT   Antinomianism. Hmm... From somewhere. Do you need a pillow behind your back? Of course you do. Here.

I   Thanks. He mentioned Hebrews 10:16. Something

about, "In those days, I will put my laws in their hearts, and write them in their minds." It's a transformation from law-centeredness to say that loving God and others fulfills the law, or shows us how to fulfill the law. "Perfect love casts out fear." He was wary of antinomianism.

LT   What about you? Pro or con?

I   On the sliding scale, I fall somewhere closer to "no law" than he does.

LT   Hippie.

I   Yeah you like it.

LT   Only hippies like you ever go to bars and meet shady guys like me.

During the pauses of my conversation with LT, I recall the fight I had years ago with my brother, Ardent.

Ille

Ard.   I don't like hanging out with you at bars.

I   What's that, Ardent? Hmm. Really? I thought tonight was actually fun for once.

Ard.   You don't care about my friends. You just try to be the center of attention. Whenever nobody is paying attention to you, you do something to get attention.

I   Get attention like how?

Ard.   Like LT. We were getting ready to leave, and you started talking to LT.

I   LT was sitting at a table by himself because your friends

42

were filling up the other table. Of course I talked to him.

Ard.   So what did you talk about?

I   I said it was nice to meet him. I said good luck in his next game. I asked what LT stands for.

Ard.   You you you. You didn't even learn anything about him.

I   He said LT stands for Lonely Table.

Ard.   You just couldn't care anything about him. You couldn't ask, "Hey, what are you like? Where are you going in life?" He's just a face in a bar.

Hic

I   It seems like just yesterday.

LT   I heard a new word today. Deliquesce. It means "to melt away." Here, it has more meanings, too. Here, read these definitions.

I   Deliquesce. Ah. "To melt away. To disappear as if by melting. To become fluid or soft on maturing, as certain fungi. To branch out into numerous subdivisions that lack a main axis, as the stem of an elm." Word.

LT   I was looking up something else at the time. I also learned a new phrase. I was watching the commentary from that movie, and the commentator used the phrase, "abstract cinema."

I   Abstract cinema! Hmm... I never thought about that. Abstract art, or abstract thought. But not cinema. That's great!

LT   Yes. The movie was abstract. And absurd.

I   Like us. Not like us. I don't know. And what about impressionism in cinema? In life and literature? Does talking about these things make us... aloof?

LT   We may be impressions since we don't exist. It has nothing to do with being aloof. Put that out of your absent mind.

Ille

I   "Where are you going in life?" Hmm... Where am *I* going in life?

Ard.   You're so far away. You're not interested in knowing others, in getting close. You're aloof. You don't care you just need to impress.

I   What can I do? What is this about?

Ard.   You're a flirt. And you were making him uncomfortable. It was obvious from his body language. The best way to interest a person is to be interested in them, not impress them.

I   What's a flirt? What aren't you telling me?

Ard.   I'm just telling you that in a bar, what you were doing was flirting. He just wanted to sit by himself.

I   Oh, are we just talking about bar etiquette? Okay, then. For a minute there you were sounding a little preachy.

Ard.   You really resist exactly this way whenever I try to teach you anything. You resist the humiliation of being taught. You refuse to learn anything.

I   I thought you just said you weren't trying to teach me things except bar etiquette.

Hic

LT   Are you familiar with Debussy? Oh, of course—we're

listening to "Voiles" right now.

I   What fills a sail? What follows a veil? I have to get comfortable. I have to lean my head against the couch like this.

LT   Do you need another pillow, then? Here is another pillow. Or would you rather lean against me?

I   How could I? Your voice lacks a body. You are made of only words. Although it would be nice in theory, we could face the same direction instead of these opposite ones.

LT   Are we facing opposite walls, then?

I   No, I think that we are facing each other. But you look at me and I look away from me. You look in and I look out.

LT   Is this an example of impressionist cinema?

I   *The Sitting Humans* is impressionist cinema.

LT   Ah, yes. And what makes it impressionistic? What is impressionism in literature?

I   This infinite white room gives the impression of a world, without a world. And then there is the black ink of dialogue.

LT   Yes, I think the dialogue makes the film an example of impressionism.

I   Actually, I was imagining the girl in the white dress walking through the camera. That seems like impressionism to me.

LT   I enjoy it in the same way that I do impressionism, somehow. I can't quite pick out anything specific other than dialogue, though. Are you familiar with Cézanne?

I   I think that possibly it's impressionism when I touch your face like this. See?

LT   Is your hand warm or cold? Did you strike or did you soothe? Oh, there's a Cézanne right in this book open between us. Let me see.

I   The color of your skin. What other films are impressionistic?

Ille

Ard.   You have no humility, which is why you don't fit in in a bar. In a bar, you have to just sit around and sometimes nobody pays attention to you, and it's humiliating. It's a lesson in meekness. Blessed are the meek, remember? Come down to earth, December, you gaudy superhero!

I   It is humiliating to be taught. It is. What do you see in me? What's wrong? What are we talking about? Superwhat?

Ard.   You are so aloof! I can't believe how unwilling you are! You melt away, there's nothing to press against. This is the last time I will ever try to explain something to you!

I   This is a difficult problem. What is the problem? This is awful.

Hic

LT   I don't know. Here is some Cézanne. I have always been struck by this one. I usually don't like still-lifes, but somehow his blotches are more interesting than someone else's blotches.

I   "Tulips in a Vase." It's fantastic. I really like this and this.

LT   The background amazes me.

I   These are interesting, too. I like this one. "Man in Belly of Lion."

LT   I like that one. Oh, that one's not even Cézanne.

I   Ooh. Do you like this?

LT   I like this more than I like Cézanne. That wall behind those dancers is a cloud. And see? There is writing on it. What does it say?

I   Those dancers are clouds. And this one is magical. "Dialogue Filling the Hollow of a Story." This is a fantastic book. I could just keep flipping through it.

LT   Stop when you want. I wanted to use this book to talk about impressionism. I used to want to talk about impressionism with this book. I want to use. I used to want.

I   Oh, we can do that.

LT   I don't remember how to. Anyway, this is better.

Ille

Ard.   You're far away looking down at us! I can't believe how aloof you are! You've evaporated. You're not even here right now!

Blank   You're right, okay? I know! I'm sorry! I don't know how to come back.

Ard.   I don't even know what deliquesce means!

Hic

I   You think about it. I'll lean on you now and flip through this book, okay? Just let me know when to stop.

LT   I forget when to stop.

Ardent worries about his machine-like sister, about how she may discover that she is a machine. Once, in a bad dream, he read the following excerpt from her journal.

I despised humans in an effort to become one. My hope was a warm mansion that I haunted, now locked up so I may squint jealously through the keyhole. In fact, this does not capture now the comprehension of my miserable fate. Every bright door closes at my arrival: a gnashing of teeth, muffled voices. All along, my self-discovery was ripening on that bough of the Tree of Knowledge while I dined (I imagined!) on nectar and ambrosia. In my memory, even the sweet stroll through Eden darkens with the umbra of that fruit.

It happened while I was preparing dinner that evening. The windows filled with dusk, and a few bulbs had burnt out among the kitchen lights, so those remaining pressed back a heavy shroud of shadows.

The confirmation of my suspicions followed. The subsequent rush from Eden was completed in the next few seconds. My cleaver slipped as I turned from slicing tomatoes and neatly impaled my right foot at the exact same moment that I screamed. This is how it happened: sparks sprang up from the wound, still housing the knife, accompanied by the sound of static and the ashen whispers of shorted circuits. I knelt to peal back the skin of my foot, revealing not bones and blood but metal and plastic. Mechanically, I pulled the knife out of my foot and set it

48

down on the linoleum floor.

Truthfully, the suspicion that I might never be human always haunted my barren frame. I am a most complicated machine, but I am wires and metal; I am ones and zeros, damned to the mimicry of soul. One zero one zero one zero.

When my eyes close, LT lifts me off of the couch and up the stairs to his bed. His neck is warm against my fingers. He knows I am human even though I say I am not. The narrator can convince her brother, Ardent, but cannot convince LT.

Ardent is driving. He passes LT's house at this moment, but Season's face is not in the golden second-story windows. The glowing shape occurs as a hollow beam in the night's dark.

"Are you deliquescing?" Name whispers as he pulls a blanket over me. "You're treasure I treasure you." I kiss his hand for the first time in my life. I open my eyes to watch him lie down. His eyes are bright in the dim room. The hallway light beams around the edges of the door.

I rest my hand on his shoulder. My eyes close, and I try to sleep. I want to learn to sleep like this, with him, but my mind is sparking. I can feel each molecule in each finger resting on his shoulder. His shoulder contains my intersection with the world. My ears compare each of his breaths with each of mine. His breath contains my intersection with the world. The story is a wind chime. I am a tremor of air, trembling in the cavity at the center of the world. This bed beneath us is a soap bubble. Now I feel weightless. I press my ear against the pillow, and the bed falls down away from me. Isaac and I continue to sleep and not sleep this way, without the laws of gravity: antinomianism.

2. how it had been: out of sight out of mind out of body
experience, the disease and symptoms of miscommunication

He is a collection of moments, a man impoverished by
manhood, by corporeal compression, by birth instead of death, by
agglution instead of diffusion.

By barely existing, his girlfriend keeps from him her
ability to oppress him. He does not withhold his oppression from
her, no he deals it steadily. Hers is the simple task of being. His
is the complex ambition of fusion, solidarity, climax, the disease
of euphoria. When he looks down into her well, his reflection
must surface. Does he assume the form arising through depths to
kiss the air? Does she fill only the blank of his shadow on the
water, her face therefore filling exactly the space left by his?
When she looks up through her well, she views his silhouette: a
fine solid black inside the circle of her vision, accompanied by a
moment of broken sky.

How many times has he fallen in, not fallen in love but
fallen through the surface of her eyes? How many times, starting
right now, will she have to reach out her hand to steady him at the
brink?

In the universe of her thoughts, the rarest, purest fear is
that possibly she sees not him through the well, but her own
reflection and the sky behind her silhouette. Her mind does not
voice this thought, it has no language for the horror. She
experiences this fear as a desperate need to clutch at near things.
How many times has she fallen in? How many times will he have

to reach out his hand to steady her at the brink?

A visage rounds the surface of a bubble. It greets her by name, but each word plummets onto her head like a heavy shoe. Where is his body? She rubs her noggin when he pauses to smile at her, innocent as a half moon. Stepping around the bubble, she swings her head against a low chandelier containing fifty candles. The face swims in the flickering light. Where is his body? She rubs her noggin while he smiles at her, innocent as a crescent moon.

He lives inside a small green pillow. He is the only one allowed in and out. In and out: another circuit. Books are allowed in but not out, as are the following things: sleep, food, love, oxygen. Actually, eating does not take place inside the pillow, but in the larger context of his apartment, his technical residence. Other things that take place in this larger context include the following: washing, sleeping beside her, touching her face, kissing her hands, saying her name, doing her do, wording her words, being her be.

She doesn't know about the pillow, the small green one. Sometimes his body stays there. Sometimes his mind drags the corporeal mess around, but sometimes his mind wanders out alone, with only his voice—nuzzling at her neck buzzling in her ears, while his body retains for firmament cottony cotton bunched inside a green cotton pillowcase. This decapitation is what the current predicament is about, though neither of them can place their finger quite on it. She thinks of the man as a balloon, or alternatively as a crescent moon.

Carolyn Chun

He is unaware of a crescendo in the depths of his eyes.

He enjoys muddling the girl betwixt the play and the punch.

Midday before lunch, dispossessed of the stuff he's composed of,

his face converses with the girl's disbelief, the girl down the well.

His mind is hungry and the sun is full. His face crosses the circle

of sky, flat cap of her gaze, her gaze with no peripheral vision.

His visage rounds the surface of a bubble, convex like the globe of

the eye. The chandelier is still aswing, its various lights tunneling

toward various vanishing points.

"It's so rare that we encounter perfection," she says.

"But what is the context?" he replies.

"'Context?'"

"What sentence precedes that and what sentence follows

that?"

"Huh?"

"You are reading out of the dictionary, aren't you?"

3. dark clouds block out stars

With what message may we approach one another to convince that we exist? That we are ourselves, who we think we are, what we may be? When words fail, then real language arrives, that rare guest. This is the only language Isaac believes in.

In the grocery store, shelves of bread, his mind is a complete blank. He's not sure how long he has waited before he sees himself standing there, glances at some of the writing on the tags and grabs a loaf. It wasn't always like this. He recalls fits of determination, clarity, focus. He feels himself turning inward, turning into Isaac the Examiner now. He's already turned on his old languagings, that empty sleeve unable to reach or touch. He leaves the bread. He drives to Houston.

She's there. Waiting.

The tongue is an unruly member, but out of the heart's abundance the mouth speaks. It's the heart that can't be reasoned with. It's the heart that reaches out to touch her name.

He has this dread that now nothing can happen. Sometimes his logic wakes up his desperation, shaking it, telling it, "I felt lonely." These moments are deceptions that he lives with.

He can live on nearly nothing. He chooses to.

The *yes* of her body pierces his silence. She is nothing like Noelle.

4. that sharp-finned

Dear Noelle,

I resemble a careening train.

I want to show you both harm and mercy. I do not want to harm you. I do not really understand what I, why I, how I, etc. You closed the door and sat down. I told you something and something etc. You are helping me understand what I did to you (here, linguistically at least, I'm taking responsibility for your emotions).

I love you, No. Go to your grave denying it, if you like, but it is and will remain a vain denial. We cannot complete what we were in the middle of. I don't know what we were in the middle of. I wish I knew what we had been in the middle of. We were stalled anyway. We remain stalled. We are off track. Off the tracks. You never really trusted me. You should have trusted me. Things would have been different. Things could have been different. Things might have been etc.

My love for you is something different. You and I have to tear through a jungle, we have to clear a path. There is newness, freshness in what's created and what's traveled through. It's a fight, a struggle, a difficult pleasure or need or passion or, yes, let's call it life. But we've lodged in the mire, tangled in undergrowth, our wheels spinning pitifully.

I haven't said I regret doing what I did. I don't know what you should do with that. I do know! I don't know. I do know! I don't know.

You speak often of contradictions that are just true.

Yours,
Isaac

Isaac either posts the letter or he doesn't.
If Isaac posts the letter, then Noelle either receives it or she doesn't.
If Noelle receives it, then she either opens the letter or she doesn't.
If Noelle opens the letter, then she either desires to read it or she doesn't.
If Noelle desires to read it, then she either knows how to read the letter, or she doesn't.
If Noelle knows how to read the letter, then she either reads it or she doesn't.

Noelle looks up from the piano. The clock has turned forward another minute without one blink from her. During the minute, she dreamt Isaac's face seen through a train windshield. *If Isaac sees her on the tracks, then he either brakes or he doesn't.*

No, he was not the careening train, though he sent the careening train. There is a fish made of glass shards hanging against the wall over the piano. The fish is dry and sharp.

No's eyes study the black and white keys beneath her fingers. Carefully, in a broken motion, one can entirely depress a piano key without exacting a note. These are the only motions she makes. Perhaps her mouth opens and closes wordlessly. Her fingers stroke the keys. She explores the space he once occupied. Her fingers stroke the keys. Not a sound. Blank stare.

I resemble a piece of glass that's been run through by a train.

Holding my breath waiting for the train; I wanted it, the wound. I'll never have to trust you now that I don't trust you. It is a horrible relief to be the victim.

I see that we'll never touch. Even this not touching you is too loud for my ears. I can't sleep through it. I can't stop saying to you. These words are your wake, breaking my mind's surface with softening ripples.

5. Look hard enough at anything to turn it into a mirror: how it is now. (I was a time delay, and you were a word.)

"Do you really expect me to keep working at this while you go on punishing and punishing me?" Isaac asks.

"Don't do the work. I don't mind. It hardly means anything to me," Noelle lies.

"I'm thinking about writing you a bill for the work that I've done."

After a delay, this is what she sings:

(I think she's still mad!)

"Be logical! Rational! Ambidextrous! Breathe underwater! Move objects such as these with your mind: heart feelings temperature time. First put them upside down! Then put them on your head! Spin them round and round! Lie down on your bed and die! There is no day like everyday (for example this one)! Write a bill for what is owed! Sign it with your name! When speaking only speak in code! She's just a photo in a frame! Let her close her eyes and ears and hit her with a train!"

"I'm embarrassed by how much I've said," she admits, not that she has said anything aloud. Not spoke nor sung nor breathed.

It stops mattering and she speaks to him again.

"What if I never mean anything to you? What if I never recover from what you do and do and do? What if I sacrifice everything that I am? What if it would be convenient for me if you stopped existing but much more satisfying if I stopped? I had no idea of what you were capable of what I was capable incapable."

Isaac adds figures on a bill. He adds and adds and adds.

Noelle doesn't feel any better. "Write me a bill because your feelings are hurt. I know I know it hurts because you treasured me so much (Noelle you're treasure I treasure you) and now gone don't I owe you don't I really."

There is a pause. Neither knows the answer to the following question.

"When will your body make me angelic?"

Carolyn Chun

6. The fish exhales: messages found inside bottles

I forget your face, except the curve of your jaw.

Can you wait any longer for me? I am stranded.

I am a strand. I am a line from your face.

This note is a sail pushed by breath. It cannot reach you.

In the middle of the day, my heart fills with white light.

This is where I am: a line of sand between pointed rocks.

The beach is shaped like a knife. I've tied

a red sail to a tree, and lean against the trunk of the tree.

I wave like a flag toward you, where I think you are.

You taste like salt. You sound like waves, water falling into

water.

I am waiting in the shade. I'll wait through the night.

As long as you'd like.

I've been here for years now.

I can see you're not coming. A gust of wind against my skin

echoes your refusal. Around the edges of sleep,

moonbeams forgive us. It's all they can do,

traveling so far through such dark.

The sea sucks sand beneath my feet:

soon I will stand on water.

When the tide comes in, you lift a bottle out.

Put this message aside.

7. She is the softest thing he'll ever touch.

For a moment, Noelle softens. This is what she tells him: "There is nothing you can do at a time like this except wait for a new time all the time. Say something sad until you cry say something normal until you're normal. Say yourself a new life and then live inside it. Make sure it is a life with a view through a glass window, maybe an aquarium, but no doors you don't know what's out there just waiting."

Noelle becomes self-conscious. "Don't speak; it will all be over soon."

Noelle's eyes deepen and resemble volcanic glass. She remembers something. "You told me once to inhabit you."

Isaac wonders who Noelle is talking to.

***

III: Gravity Levity

1. the words they don't say, the looks in the same direction

The voice opens. The voice in love ascended too quickly in pitch. Now it sinks back down from the rafters as the temperature goes out of the house. Cold ecstasy the voice exhales from the stone floor, braiding together its streams and flights and shards of glass. It, aground, is unsure how much further it will fall. It mends what it has, putting all of the parts into what it will now be, what it now is here, at this level perspective. When the voice opens, blood spills. When the voice closes, it gently expires. The voice is meager and meek, wretched and resonant, terrible and terrified. Where is its home? It is undressed asleep on the floor. It will not leave until you crack open the door.

For example, he cracked open. He was its residence just now, a house of mirrors dressed like windows. In what form will he return? The sound of ascending steps? The key tapping on the windshield of a car? Light the color of wheat around the edges of the door? A chain-link fence? A feather? A marble? The voice prefers to inhabit a warm, expansive house. An upturned face. The voice prefers to regard the sky, the chiseled stars.

2. It might rain.

She wants a man to lift her into the air. She has left no part of herself unbroken in search of him.

He would like to lift her up and gently set her down. No, he will hold her until the burning stops. No, she will want to be let go. He will not touch her at all then. He looks down and away, embarrassed.

She won't stop until she's completely exhausted. She won't stop until she's down to the bone. She won't stop until the bone shatters. Her obsidian eyes are melting. They sink back into the molten rock. She is melting into a pool of magma at the center of the earth.

He closes his eyes. He doesn't see. He wonders if she'll strike him. If she'll dance on his broken bones. If she'll touch him. If her touch will feel broken, like glass. She has broken like glass.

She has never been so infinitesimal. She has never been so small. Through the ceiling she beholds the wakened stars: that unrecovered landscape. Amen. Amen.

He will look at her. He will touch her face. He will do whatever she wants. It can begin again. He will hold onto the broken glass. His eyes are closed. He doesn't see.

Her form bleeds molecules. Is she dividing the harvest? She isn't glass. She isn't stone. She isn't melted. He doesn't see: she is invisible. She tells him to leave.

Don't leave.

She tells him she'd like him to leave.

Please don't leave.

She would like very much for him to leave now.

He sees her through the window. She is already outside, popping the stars one by one like packaging bubbles. Soon it is dark, and he will not see.

She touches the closed window. The cool glass touches her.

Carolyn Chun

3. empty spaghetti sauce jar

When you talk to me like this I almost can't even hear you,
you are a great distance away, and your lips flit like the blank
wings of a moth,
I puzzle over what grows there, in your sallow voice,
even as I'm listening to you say these words I know that
I'll never understand what you mean, you old grub,
in fact, when you said the blank wings of a moth,
I began to concentrate on the white lips of your mouth opening
and closing.
Next, I imagined the thin wings of a moth, soft as air,
then a blazing white field, shining grasses and white tissue
blossoms blinding at midday,
moths at their lips,
then a glisten and a shiver, and the field parts down the middle,
a black lightning crack splits the ground,
and then the interruption of words.

4. not filled with lightning

      "Can you close the door and sit down? Something bad," he says. Her bedroom door soft and ight shut smooth as the curve of a cheek. His eyes are bright and sharp as lion's teeth.

5. Underneath is what the up there was.

      Endless aqua waves pitch against endless white sand. This place is precarious: recall how perfectly sand fills an hourglass. Through palm trees, the sun has set or else not yet risen. The sky hovers kindling a gray hope or else quenching the final embers, striking a single, minor chord.

      Imagine lifting a small piece of a destroyed thing. Father took an axe to the piano. Downward slashes on the upright piano; the upturned face continues to not blink. Bits of ivory—or is it plastic—and dark wood flew everywhere. Somehow dust has managed to coat the whole room. The thin wood from the sheet music holder is in many pieces. I lift one the size of my little finger from the wrecked keyboard and drop it back onto the pile where it hits with a *tack*.

      Icicles cling to the window. Outside, somebody has cleared out a rectangle of snow to dig a grave. The light comprehends this and illuminates a low cloud. The light from the sky is both obtuse and shallow.

      Now the waves come shouting up onto the shore, grasping a near palm tree by its base. The water and sky are the color of smoke.

      At night, an avalanche swallows the sky. The house

responds to the snow as a piano responds to an axe. The only survivor is the man in the grave. I pound on the roof of the cave. I press my shoulder against the lid of this box. *Hello?* It is very dark in here. Pure darkness beneath a white mountain of snow, clear ice crystals, and a moonless night above.

The sea glitters icily. The sun breaks open on my face. Startled, golden light flashfloods the still air. The gray sky lifts from the world like a lace tablecloth. Or it falls away like a tissue wing. Blue diamonds fill the water. Music empties the sky.

Pressed into the black contours I have dug, I consider the places I have intended to go. I recall a painting over the piano of Hawai'i: leaning palm trees, volcanic sand and sky, aqua water. When the lid lifts to blinding light, I know that I have fallen asleep and dreamt because I wake up. *Found one still moving.* Two orange-vested excavators pull me shivering to my feet.

6. She stares at a... made from pieces of broken... Why does the mirror break? Whose reflection is in pieces? Nothing? Nothing.

Once upon a time there was a beautiful in a faraway. Her hair was. Her eyes were. The tender roll of her voice broke his. The visiting prince began to weep for. Her voice reminded him of. He loved. He knelt, pressed a kiss to her hand, and asked if she loved. Her were eyes heavy with sorrow, and she said. When her father, the king, heard of the man's proposal, he banished the visiting prince from the. The king had been bewitched by the evil. The princess herself was under a, and only human during the. Every evening she became, instead of her natural form, a terrible. Every evening, at sundown, she spread her and flew to the rafters of the bell tower just outside of the kingdom to wait until. From the high beams, she sang all night, as her voice was her only human. The tower was said by all the townspeople to be. The prince, banished from the kingdom, wandered along its edges, sick with. The prince was under a spell, too, but not a spell of the evil. He came upon an old bell tower covered with cobwebs and. The sun was just setting, but he was weary with sadness, having traveled many miles from the princess whom he. He lay beside the tower, covered himself with his cape, and. Presently it was dark, and the woods close by became alive with skittering noises and howls and terrible. The prince awoke and drew his sword, though his eyes were filled with. He heard a stirring above him, in the top of the bell tower, and he looked up, but in the dark he could see. And then from the tower, a voice began to. The song was as pure as. It contained the infinite grief of the ocean, and the crystalline perfection of the on a clear. The prince thought he must be dreaming, or possibly in his grave, to be hearing so distinctly the voice of the beautiful, who was far away in her father's. The song also soothed the creatures of the night who had been stirring in the dark. The creatures came to the edge of the clearing containing the bell tower to listen to the. The coyote stretched out beside the rabbits, and the asp coiled up beside a. He realized that there was to fear that. The prince set down his and lay down again beside the, his heart.

7. I suffocate in an empty room. I am simple and ordinary.

yes no

I you

a little left

unmakes me still

face for face

breath for breath

it must be you

taking me away with you

don't return

but now you are coming back

i make you

by scratching in the dust in the dark

but i am made from you,

i am an arch of your rib, some tissue,

and i grow, make room to hold this memory

what is left—what is here—what i will escape—what escapes

me—what I am now.

i grow. i make room. to hold this memory.

we met. something. is missing.

we married in the long corridors of an airport.

no. no, of course not.

we met in the long, full corridors of an airport. how long ago

something is missing. it may be all we have to go on.

i dragged an enormous black suitcase. with tiny wheels. a stuffed duffle bag over my shoulder. the clasp snapped suddenly, right there in the middle of a crowd of rushing people. The clasp to the strap on my suitcase. Did the suitcase jam against a door? Or a foot? I remember now exactly how I felt at that moment, how my entire life narrowed down to the space of that instant. Suffocating. Waves of people.

Where was I? Why was I going away? Something is wrong.

As I stood there, staring blankly at the ruined strap, as passengers shoved past me, my stomach tensed. My throat tightened. My eyes burned and watered behind my dark sunglasses. My vision blurred. I was dizzy, drowning. And then removed. It was as if time slowed, and I looked down on someone else's hands from a cool, open space, miles away. Was it a moment later, or several minutes when you, passing by, you lifted my suitcase by the handle without stopping or even slowing down? I watched your nebulous silhouette stride before a beaming window, orange. Or is that my foggy memory? You lifted my suitcase without even slowing down.

You took me away. I was never the same. Or am I the same? Now, am I just the same? No, something is missing. You wouldn't recognize me now.

You wouldn't recognize me because you've been away for so long. Or am I away? Do you want to know what I am now? It's strange—I've been writing this a long time. Days? I was just a lump then, when I began, a fleshy bend inching around the keyboard, pressing, so deliberately, key after key. I was unrecognizable. I was a strip of tissue, a few vertebrae and part of a rib.

And now? Well, I'm growing. I remember—and how is it I remember, being such a diminishment?—when I first noticed the alteration. I went into the bathroom to cut my nails. It was early—the morning after that last night together.

The small bathroom was dim. Dappled light filtered through the dark blue curtain over the high window. And, as I began to dig through my mom's little box of hair things and whatnots looking for the cutters, I noticed that my nails were already short. I didn't then think of my nail ends as *missing*, of course. I assumed that I'd forgotten about trimming my nails the night before. It would have been hard for me to notice something as small as cutting my fingernails that night.

And then I disappeared. It was gradual, and incapacitating. I found this place to make a record of my final hours. But I am sightless, unable to read this, as unable as you are. And now I am growing. I have a spine, small hips, and two antennae-like arms, which make the typing easier. My memory stretches back to find us. So, now I must see what I am, what you are. I recall a beginning. Oh, yes. Where we were. The airport. Here we are.

As I stood there, staring blankly at the ruined strap, as passengers shoved past me, I felt absent and present at the same time. You lifted my suitcase by the handle without stopping or even slowing down. Then, you carried it off, leaning slightly to the right as the suitcase bounced against your left leg in motion. And what about me?

I followed you to an airport café, a counter and a few tables by a large window. Planes landed and took off under a coral sunset sky. You hefted my bag up onto a rickety chair and turned to me, following absently. You, no passenger, you, in your captain's hat and sunglasses and wings. You are coming into focus. With one motion, you slid off your shiny sunglasses and hung them on the pocket of your shirt, over your wings, beside your navy blue tie with the fish print. Were those fish moving? Swimming the contours of the knot? Of course not. Your uniform, your suit and tie and hat, were all navy blue. I'm remembering. Undressed, your face was beautiful—did I know it then?—your eyes dark brown and playful, your face flushed and halfway smiling, halfway serious. You looked clean and perfect, with your hat resting on your dark crew cut. You were

"Isaac," you said, sticking out your hand. Your voice was clean and sweet. "Captain Isaac," you added, smiling brightly. Your teeth were sharp and white. It was the year we turned twenty-five.

"Captain," I began, taking your hand, "I'm Noelle. Thanks so much for your help. I didn't know what I; I mean, I thought... well, I couldn't think... Strange, I..." You squeezed my hand and looked me in the eye. After a moment, you looked away, blushing wonderfully again.

"Oh. You'd have thought of something." I'll admit that I

wondered then if you'd fly me out of that world. You squatted to look at my broken clasp while I set down my duffle with a *thump*. "So where are we off to? Someplace special?" You pulled the strap out of my hand and began to thread it through the remaining ring of the broken clasp.

"Oh, I'm going home. I was teaching inner city public school with this program. Physics. I don't really know why I even went. The drugs and the *noise*. A note ringing in my ears. Tinnitus."

"Well… it's only October. Maybe you'd like it if you got used to it some more. But… maybe not. What do you want to do, anyway?" the Captain asked, sliding the strap through itself again into a new handle and testing it with a few tugs.

"Well, I'm through with getting used to that school for now. I want to do something exciting, you know. How about if I run away and become a pilot."

You smiled again. "Actually, that does sound like a great idea, now that I think about it. Well, that or joining the circus. Maybe I can help." Is this right?

"Oh, I couldn't ask you for anything," I joked, ready to ask for everything.

"Well, who would you ask?" Your eyes here. The way you looked at me.

"Well, but I don't even... And you've already—" I looked down, speechless. My need was so blatant. I was no help to myself.

"Sometimes I think you don't even know me," you

responded. Or no. It wasn't that at all. You really said something corny. "Getting you off the ground! That's what a pilot does!" You may have saluted at the end.

"Yes, getting away is one part. And coming back down is the other."

"Yes, that's the bit one should learn first."

"Well, thanks for your help."

"It was nothing, Noelle, just a little luggage trick. Let me buy you a drink. Unless you're, that is, if you have some time right now." You blushed a little then, and I was so grateful. Grateful for your charm. For your attention. For your nervousness.

You bought me a pineapple juice and we talked until my final boarding call. I told you everything. Well, I told you what everything was to me then: why I left the school, what I was expecting at home with my parents, what was wrong with me. So long ago. I hated to complain to you, we'd just met, but I couldn't stop *saying*.

And you, you listened so wonderfully to me. You insisted that everything was about to get better, like waking up from a bad dream. You gave me the impression of a new world, your world. You told me about your hometown of Atlanta. You were a new pilot. I noticed then that you were just trying to get away, too. You loved the sky and all of its colors up there and missed it when you were below the clouds. We were so young, then. It even seemed strange to me then that we had met only then, that I hadn't known you until that day. And what does it mean that you rescued me? That you were the doorway to a new life? What does it mean that now I want to escape?

That all seems so far away. Does that sound heartless and distant? I write and grow. Bone fibers sprout and harden—I can *feel* them somehow—and muscle and nerve and skin bundle about them. I have cartilage between my vertebrae and I have one lung and over half of the mate. But I'm growing even faster, now. I almost feel a weak throbbing in my chest. It certainly must be my old heart! I'm feeling alive. I feel like I might almost be somebody. I'm finally awake after a very long time.

This distance I feel between myself and my story: Who is Isaac and who is Noelle? Am I the pilot or the nervous flight? From somewhere, from a long way off, the story returns.

I fell asleep and dreamed about you on that plane ride home after meeting you. My anxieties about my parents' disappointment had melted away during our brief conversation, and had been replaced with the hope of you, even just the idea of you. The plane landed in Charlotte, but I was ready to take off for Atlanta in the same moment. You wouldn't invite me over right away, but I hardly remember those weeks—were they months?— at home that dragged on except for the few times a week when you called and my heart leaped up into the nighttime sky. I can't quite reconstruct that time, that nothing time like an ellipsis between words.

How to Break Article Noun

You got me a job as a flight attendant, a job I hated but that kept me close to you. Now I see that I couldn't have been a pilot. My parents encouraged me to keep the job. They didn't know about you yet. I knew and I didn't know.

My first flight took me out to Atlanta, your hometown, where you met me for dinner. Even without your suit and hat, you were the Captain. You met me at the gate with lavender irises. You held my hand. Downtown in your favorite restaurant, we schemed together to end up in the same cities at the same times. You knew all the scheduling tricks. You knew everything, then. I followed you anywhere.

We met next in New York, and I noticed my voice had been stretched tight at the distance between us, relaxing only at the sight of you. After that, we met for dinners in our matching uniforms in a dozen neon cities. Bit by bit we built that new wing of our lives. We *believed* in it, that web we laid of flights between all the major cities in the continental United States. And then that first weekend we spent in Chicago.

When I think about that weekend, our stay in the Four Seasons Hotel, our adventures downtown, you hailing a cab in the rain, the water everywhere as if the very air was melting. When I think about falling asleep with the bed miles beneath us, I feel in love all over again with that young man, Captain. I'd like to stop this story right here right now, with my hand in yours, and you leaning forward in the street full of headlights and red lights and blue steel rain. I'd like to stop right here with my hair clinging to my skin, my face dripping and cold, my coat and dress soaked through. I'd like to stop shivering, my hands wrapped, now, around your free arm. I'd like to stop with your arm bent into the rain-filled air. Let's be this liquid let's deliquesce.

Or, better still, let's stop in the first cab that pulled up, spraying us, headlights framing your silhouette for a moment. Let's stop right here in the cab, with your hand on my neck, your fingertips mesmerizing my skin. Let's stop at the wink of dialogue we shared, my head resting on your soaked shoulder, your arm, now, around my shoulders as you look at me and ask

"Are you tired?" pushing the hair away from my face. "How could I be? My life's a dream."

I can't pause any longer. Was it a moment or several minutes that I leaned back from the keyboard? Now I feel the disappearance encroaching, Captain, untying my new knots. I have fallen out of the story again, out of my memories. What does it mean to be a torso with a spine and two nearly-formed arms? And what does it mean to be a set of hips? Parts of legs and a stump of neck? I'm going to be whole, somehow. I can see it now. How I will be. When I'm done with escape. I guess we now see that this writing is all that I am, so I should give up what I used to be, that other self. So different from who I am now.

A year later, you proposed to me in Vegas. Elvis married us. We told my family later, right after getting pregnant. We bought a house in a little suburb of Charlotte, close to my parents. I left the airline. I spent a lot of time with my parents while you went flying around the country, and the rest of the time I spent in our new home, decorating. Especially Susanna's new room. I missed the excitement of new cities with you, moving in your wake, but the endorphins flooding my system kept me aglow with every promise from you. Every week with you at its end. Every day with you around the corner. Every hour bending your flight back to me.

Your absences seemed to grow longer. Your features sharper. Were you flying farther and farther away? No, of course not! The trips were not different from our old flight patterns. Still, those fish dancing on your tie with those neat turns at the edges of the fabric became frantic. I didn't let it bother me.

Instead, I sat on a stool to stencil blue numbers and pink alphabet letters around Susanna's yellow room. Yellow as a duckling. Yellow as a daisy. Yellow as the school bus that would take Susanna to and from kindergarten as, day by day, Susanna overturned my lonely-for-you life with her bright charm and attention and need. Yellow as the dress she wore on her first day of first grade.

She studied the sky through the windshield as I drove.

"Mom, what if I don't like school? What if the girls don't like me?" Susanna refused to befriend boys categorically. It might have been because she saw so little of you, her pilot daddy who played airplane with her and sang "Oh, Susanna" to her. Of course she loves you dearly. She has your bright, open face, a little chubbier, your startling smile, your shy assertiveness, your soft brown hair. Oh Susanna, Susanna don't you cry, with my blue eyes. She didn't trust you. Or, no, that was later. I'm getting ahead of myself again. She didn't distrust you. I hardly distrusted you. She missed you. She didn't understand your flights like I did. For her, it was out of control. She didn't see the pattern in it, the promise that the sky held for us.

There she was in my front seat, our wisp of a girl in her favorite yellow dress.

"Susanna, if any of those girls don't like you, they're crazy! You know, I'm crazy about you. It's going to be harder for *you* to like all of *them*," I assure her, squeezing her hand. "Anyway, if you don't like your school, then we will have to go live on a deserted island with Captain and never go to school again."

"Sometimes I think you don't even know him," she responded, turning to the window. No! Of course she didn't say that. I can't seem to stay on pace. No, Susanna brightened when I talked about her father.

"Yes! Let's go do that!" she said. "And we'll bring Gram an' Poppy. And a puppy."

"We'll do whatever we want. It'll be like in our dreams." I stop by the flagpole in front of the red brick building and suddenly worry for her at the sight of bigger, tougher kids standing around and walking in crowds. I feel nervous. My grip tightens on the steering wheel. My mind races. "Suz, you know, you don't have to go in today, if you don't want to. You can come back home and keep your mom company and help make cookies!" The thought of the empty house and Susanna's first whole day of school lasting until 3pm is a sudden shock. I'm not sure in this instant what to do for her.

"Oh, Mom! We're already here!" Susanna says with a big smile, noticing her friend, Julie, knocking on her window. Susanna's already familiar with my moods and worries. She knows how to make me feel silly for worrying. "I'll see you later." She stretches up for a kiss and slides out of the car, dragging her backpack out of the foot space. How perfectly she copies your smile!

I watch her until she passes through the double doors of the school, swept away by currents of children. I go for a drive through town along the river. A plane growls overhead, reminding me of you.

When I get home, your credit card statement is in the mail. Confirmation. Why am I surprised when the illusion ends? You can get off the ground, can't you, Captain? But you never really come down. But I knew and didn't know better. I feel absent and present at the same time. I see with startling clarity that I have no control over this, any of this. I feel suddenly heavy and sit down on the floor with a *thump*.

It's the hotel charge in Houston. You've been there a little too frequently. I study the bills from that city. Pricey hotels. Meals expensive enough for two. A new student, Captain? Just as lonely as I? Just as confused? The figures blur and there's a noise in our house, I notice, like in that school I left years ago. That same note. Does she want to run away and be a pilot? Will you lift her off? I'm not up there with you anymore. I'm down on the ground. What's wrong with me?

You came home that weekend, Captain, kissing me hello. Your dark figure before the bright sunrise was framed by the doorway as I leaned close. I wondered if you would smell different, if I would taste guilt on your lips. You called Suzie, and she ran in from the kitchen, wrapping her arms around your leg.

"You're home again!" she cried.

"Oh, come on, Susanna! I'm always right there outside your window, flying around in the clouds, remember?" you replied, lifting her into the air.

When you spun her giggling in her soft pajamas, you were not perfect. Your edges had gone all sharp. I noticed some premature gray in your soft hair. Some wrinkles around your eyes. I'll admit it. I wondered if there was anything you could do. I wanted you to lift me up and stop the note ringing, grating on my mind. But you looked altogether tired—well you should, working as you'd been. The buzz, I finally realized, was the spinning inside my atoms. I was coming apart. I felt suddenly exposed, both to you and by you. My arms were planes of a revolving door. How could we have ever met, each being made of such empty space? You passed through and left me spinning, and you were not perfect as you should have been. The fish were at the edges of your tie, then, trying to swim through the seams. Our daughter didn't know you. You were stealing from us with your flight, with your Houston, with your making us love you. Susanna touched your face as if she could snatch off a piece of you to keep. Oh, how she loves you! It wasn't until you asked

"What's wrong, Sweetheart?" that I noticed I was crying. Tears dripping onto my nightgown.

I need to remember this part. The difficulty of breathing. The frantic soundlessness.

And now, I am growing growing growing. I'm not there in that cramped living room. My legs have ankles and feet, and my hands are complete down to the fingernails. I keep touching my neck and head. My left ear has just now cracked open to the sounds of my typing. It's so wonderful! The air sounds fresh. It's clean as water. I would smile and laugh out loud except that my face is still a blank slate. I feel like jumping up and down! Oh, every sound is like food to me, every press of the keyboard, every beat of my heart. I knock on the desk, I slide my chair; I'd like to sing. I cover my ear and uncover it again and again, so grateful.

But the story is waiting. We started this flight and now

we must land.

That night, I felt disconnected from our bed when I lay down. I felt invisible. Placeless. You were already asleep, so I woke you. As if you could have helped me.

"Isaac, how was Houston?" I asked, staring blankly at the ceiling.

"Hmm?" you asked, turning your head on the pillow, your eyes slicing open. You yawned. "Let's talk tomorrow, honey, mmm? When you can shut the door and sit down?"

You turned to me smiling and touched my cheek with the backs of your fingers. When you touched me, I wanted to escape. It was strange, you touched my skin and I felt empty. I wondered if you would cry.

"Flying around is your life."

"Noelle, let's talk about this in the morning. I'm home now, okay? We can talk about everything tomorrow. C'mon, Sweetheart," you said, grabbing my shoulders, holding me in your arms because, by then my voice was choked up. "C'mon, No, just go to sleep, just go to sleep for now. Shhhh. Shhhh. Has your mind been making things true, again? Hmm?" The noise, the soft pitch, enlarged the space between us. My entire life narrowed down to the space of your whisper. You kissed my face and I was still. More still than I'd ever been. I knew then what I realize again now. Your betrayal was taking me apart. You've made me disappear. In our room that night, I was as still as a corpse.

How to Break Article Noun

It all happens again as I type. With these closed eyes of mine, I see you leaning over me. I don't have much further to go, though. Yes, I'm almost done with this. Let's see what I am about to be. By now, I have toes to wiggle. I scratch an itch on my neck. I flare my nostrils and run my tongue along my teeth and lips. I'm almost myself again! I wonder if this growing will produce something new in me, sharper hearing, night vision, fangs. I'm starving, I realize. Of course I am: I haven't eaten in days!

You fell asleep with your head on my belly. I slid out of your bed and packed up some clothes. I drove here to my parents' house, beneath the coral sky. They've been gone; they haven't seen me disappear being here. They haven't seen how you've made me not matter, how we can't touch, how impossible it all was. Yes, now my eyelids tear open. This screen is blinding white. I can't read a word on it. I look down, though, and my whole body is glowing. But this is a new body, an unspotted one. I flex my muscles. You are absent and I am finally present. It's true that I've been yours for years. Now, though, every inch of my skin is tingling. I'm going to use this body to lift off. I'll be the one to take flight, Isaac. I'll never come apart again. I'm going to keep this body. I feel like I have wings.

***

IV: The Accidental Essay

1. What fills a sail? What follows a veil?

What's missing here may be all we have to go on. (Remaining content has passed over the event horizon.) At the center of everything, a little girl. At the center, Susanna, asking.

"Why are we down in the (primordial) ooze, Mommy?" Why must we always begin from chaos, Suz? The broken-down pieces of my genetic code swarm among dense clouds of animated possibilities. I am trying to decipher the codes. I am constructing a translation and interpretation in the earliest fires—the magma underlying every step toward the made thing, the shimmering obsidian I desire to break in my hands. What is it I desire to quench? What am I able to destroy?

"Why does Daddy have to go away so much?"

Thermodynamics informs us of the universal tendency towards disorder. Therefore, the initial conglomeration of amino acids that precipitated the congealing of a human face may be a highly organized system that has merely degenerated into this, her current planet. Diversification is disorganization from the perfect order of the quantum void preceding the Big Bang. The second law of thermodynamics is the elegant admission of the tendency of all things to break down. Desire for ruin is the law.

2. Tulips in a Vase

"What noise, Mommy?"

Matter is empty. Matter is composed of atoms, which are composed of electrons, protons, and neutrons in a vacuum: a few marbles in a bare room. I study Isaac—he is empty space. The hand has its various parts: bone, vein, muscle, skin, etc. The part has its cells. What exists to desire? The cell has its molecules, and each molecule its atoms.

"Would you carry me? I'm getting tired, Mom."

Our atoms do not meet, my little Fuzzy; hence hand does not meet hand. I pick her up. She lays her head on my shoulder. Two bodies pressed together do not physically meet. My body is a blank. His body is a. Inside an atom, the nuclear forces keep the electrons at a distance from the nucleus, even though the two objects are oppositely charged. Electromagnetic forces govern interatomic interactions, the electromagnetic repulsion produces the sensation of contact between two fingers pressed together, Susanna, oh Susanna don't you cry.

Cyclotrons can accelerate particles to relativistic speeds, allowing an electron to overcome the strong force and to strike a proton in a nucleus. This collision can produce a neutron. In a neutron star, the intense gravitational pressure collapses all of the atoms of the star, so that all of the electrons collide with the nuclear protons, forming neutrons.

"What will enable our collision?" she yawns. Do I desire to be diffused, calm, neutralized?

Neutrons, protons, and electrons are composed of quarks, however. Atoms may appear to meet, but their constituents do not. But here you are, Susanna.

3. Your voice lacks a body.

"Am I too heavy?" Susanna's eyes are closed. She mumbles into my shoulder.

The force of gravity on particles is called weight. Particles do not have weight apart from the force of gravity. Gravity is an attractive force between objects that have mass. Some particles experience the sensation of mass. Particles that *have* mass "derive their mass (and thus their energy) from a dark field that fills the universe." [Preuss 2006]. (I use my cartoon physicist voice.) Physicists call this field a Higgs field, and the particle that propagates this field a Higgs boson. Physicists do not know what a Higgs boson is, Fuzzy. The potential of the Higgs field when plotted on a graph resembles the inside of the bottom of a wine bottle, where the *location* of the particle is considered to be at the center, the highest point of the mass distribution. "'That's the hell we are in,' says [theoretical physicist Hitoshi] Murayama, 'the bottom of the bottle.'" [Preuss 2006]. (I use the cartoon voice again. Susanna giggles.)

"Does this story have a happy ending?" Susanna mumbles.

Shh, Fuzzy. Of course, my love. You are all we ever had. Shh...

The Higgs field seems to behave like a Bose-Einstein Condensate. A BEC is a collection of particles, such as atoms, cooled to a temperature below some critical temperature, which behave as a single wavelike entity, a "quantum liquid" with peculiar properties. Liquid helium, a BEC, defies gravity to climb out of any container it's put into because it somehow *knows* that, outside the container, it can reach a lower potential energy.

"Apparently we are living in a Bose-Einstein Condensate in which all particles are immersed. If we turned it off, mass would vanish and everything would fly apart in a nanosecond," Hitoshi Murayama said in an interview. [Preuss 2006]. Nobody has ever found a Higgs boson. The problem of the Higgs boson is intimately related to the question of the origin of the universe.

Mass is an illusion, just as weight is an illusion, just as physical contact is an illusion. We cannot touch molecules. We are weightless, unable to touch our cold feet down.

4. The infinite white room gives the impression of a world, without a world. And then there is the black ink of dialogue.

The Milky Way Galaxy swims in the tidal forces of a supermassive black hole. Susanna rubs her eyes and yawns.

"Won't everything get sucked into the black hole, then? In the end?"

Well, my little Fuzzy, "in the classical theory black holes can only absorb and not emit particles. However, it is shown that quantum mechanical effects cause black holes to create and emit particles… This leads to a slow decrease in the mass of the black hole and to its eventual disappearance: any primordial black hole of mass less than about 10^{15} g would have evaporated by now." [Hawking 1975]. The dissipation of energy from a black hole is known as Hawking Radiation.

"Do black holes die, Mommy?"

Black holes do die.

A black hole possesses an event horizon, its limit of no return. Sometimes the universe spontaneously creates a particle-antiparticle pair just to watch them annihilate. The universe lends some theoretical energy intending to collect. Hawking radiation occurs when a particle-antiparticle pair is created at the event horizon of a black hole, and one of the pair is captured while the other escapes. Since they didn't annihilate, the universe is owed some energy. In order to fill the energy hole, energy tunnels out of the black hole and amazingly crosses the event horizon. To an outside observer, this looks like a particle being emitted. An amazing, thin-aired escape! The particle-antiparticle pair is represented by only half of the pair, though an entire black hole can dissolve by this method. Can movement continue without the wound?

"When a black hole dies, then, what about everything that's already, you know, gone into there? What happens to it? How do we even know what it was?"

The opposite reveals its lack. The visible reveals the invisible. Isaac you are so far away, as if one dead in the bottom of a tomb. I carry your design. Particle antiparticle. Making unmaking. Participle antiparticiple.

5. You look at me and I look away from me.

Albert Einstein's theory of relativity describes time dilation and length contraction between inertial reference frames moving at relativistic speeds: speeds close to the speed of light. An observer standing still is passed by a 100-meter train traveling at half the speed of light will see a train that is about 87 meters long.

"Is there a train, Mommy?"

Yes, Fuzzy. There is a beautiful train!

"Choo choo!" She turns her head on my shoulder and continues her slow breaths.

Also, while the man at rest experiences 100 seconds, a man on the train will experience only about 87 seconds. The relationship between the time experienced by the still observer, t, and the moving observer, t_m, is governed by the following equation, where v is the speed of the train and c is the speed of light.

$$ t = \frac{t_m}{\sqrt{1 - v^2 / c^2}} $$

For the man speeding on the train, the increased speed slows his experience of the progression of time. The speed of light is the only constant. Light is the constant. Light shines in the darkness and the darkness comprehends it not. It all comes down to perspective, Fuzzy, your reference frame.

The bright white, the lit page.

6. Does talking about these things make us?

      Isaac, can the space between us be crossed? Is language the tool for this? Affection? Singing? Contact must overcome an impossible gap between minds. Physics is metaphor here, and adequate symbol. Love, I am a scientist. I am a love scientist. Susanna snores softly. I keep walking in circles, her weight in my arms the only tangible (intangible) thing.

      Ezra Pound said, "The natural object is always the *adequate* symbol." [Pound 1918]. An interest in science is usually an interest in metaphor, you see, Fuzzy. Physics, chemistry, biology, and mathematics give descriptions for the microscopic world that correspond to the macroscopic world, the world of my vantage.

      Yeats encourages the symbolism of the sciences, the systematic language that lends form to formlessness. "An emotion does not exist, or does not become perceptible and active among us, till it has found its expression, in color or in sound or in form, or in all of these, and because no two modulations or arrangements of these evoke the same emotion, poets and painters and musicians, and in a less degree because their effects are momentary, day and night and cloud and shadow, are continually making and unmaking mankind." [Yeats 1900].

      Science describes the world. The world is motion and emotion. The world exists, Isaac, though no two people inhabit the same world, no two people touch. No person knows of what he is composed. "It is indeed only those things which seem useless or very feeble that have any power." [Yeats 1900]. We come apart in a nanosecond.

7. What is a tremor of air?

The human being is hollow. Your heart has its various parts: veins, blood, valves, etc. The part has its cells. The cell has its vacant atoms. So what does touch mean? Can the space between humans be crossed? How do your parts compose you, Isaac? Your sounds words movements silence silence? Shh, Susanna: Susanna don't you cry.

Among musical instruments, the cello has a pitch range closest to that of a human voice. It may be that only a mimic can perfect the human voice. Draw a bow along the string to vibrate the air, shivering your eardrum. Sound is a vibration of the inner workings of your ear. Sound acts on your ear, Isaac, the hollow it fills, the cavity, the birthplace. Music is not a tide that you move through, but a voiceless trembling of the air, a disembodied stirring just inside your skull. The one sound that you hear is the interpretation of all of the air's vibrations, bounded by the limits of your physical capacity. There are voices finer and coarser than you are able to comprehend, that your ear cannot even imagine.

The cup of an ear collects more than it can know. Remove one sound, another previously unheard replaces it. Consider that our auditory capacities can hear the rhythm of a voice, stippled with words, which our brain must interpret simultaneously. "The purpose of rhythm, it has always seemed to me, is to prolong the moment of contemplation, the moment when we are both asleep and awake, which is the one moment of creation, by hushing us with an alluring monotony, while it holds us waking by variety, to keep us in that state of perhaps real trance, in which the mind liberated from the pressure of the will is unfolded in symbols." [Yeats 1900].

In the perfect dark, the perfect still dark, he hushed her by opening up her shadow so that she climbed further and further into his mind and body, particularly his mouth, breath, and words, while he held her waking by his touch, to keep her in that state of perhaps real trance, in which the mind liberated from the pressure of the will is unfolded in symbols. His capacity in her life is to prolong the moment of contemplation. Also, she loves him. Or did. She doesn't know. Who is he even when she is away?

What's missing here may be all we have to go on.

A wind chime is a hollow containing wind. Wind vibrates in the blank tube to create pitch: music. Final test: *wind* is to *wind chime* as *blank* is to *human being*.

References:

Hawking, S. W. 1975. Particle Creation by Black Holes. *Commun. math. Phys.* 43:199.

Preuss, Paul. 2006. Looking Toward TeV. Berkeley, CA: Science@Berkeley Lab.

Pound, E. 1918. A Retrospect. In: *Poetry in Theory*, ed. Cook, J. Malden, MA: Blackwell Publishing Ltd.

Yeats, W. B. 1900. The Symbolism of Poetry. In: *Poetry in Theory*, ed. Cook, J. Malden, MA: Blackwell Publishing Ltd.

***

V: Relativity

1. She stares at a… made from pieces of broken… Forget
everything I've said before.

the color of leaves
choose others, shadows and light
choose one to be real

day, shadow of light
shadow of an eye, of a
shadow of a leaf

glass shatters the light
glass breaks glass, glass breaks an eye
this is how to slip

how does an eye break?
light shatters on crimson leaves
an eye breaks

2. the past again (a mirage)

I touch you to brush against the world.
I touch you to wake the molecules of my skin.
I inhabit the space of our meeting.
I duck out of my meager frame

to touch the molecules of your skin. To
know an eye that isn't mine or yours,
we duck out of our meager frames.
I've covered you with my eyelids.

Now an I that isn't yours or mine
inhabits the space of our meeting.
Voice is covered with eyelashes.
Opens to brush against the world.

3. Yes, No. Meditation on love stories.

The music of the Sirens destroyed grateful men. Sailors wrecked their ships on shoals and cliffs to draw near the beautiful voices. Passing by the Sirens' island, Jason and the Argonauts turned toward the shoals, leaning forward. The singing rocked over the water like an immense dream. Orpheus set down his oar and lifted his lyre. It is recorded that Orpheus played music more beautiful than the Sirens' song, saving his ship and crew. It is not recorded that the voice of his lyre knelt down before the Sirens and then arose, opening like a blossom. Nor is it recorded that Eurydice, the youngest of the Sirens, heard Orpheus and forgot how to sing, so piercing was that note. She cast herself into the water to reach his ship. She drowned in the rising voices.

Why did Orpheus look at Eurydice? Leading her away from Hades, when the price of looking at her was her life, why did he turn back? How did he feel when he saw that it was her? His eyes filling already with her departure?

Isaac stares at Noelle. "Close the door and sit down. I have something bad." Noelle knows about Erinýes in Houston. Isaac loved Noelle even when he wanted to love Erinýes. Now that he wants to love Noelle, he loves Erinýes. He knows about death waiting. If Isaac doesn't know whom he's holding; if he turns to look… If it is Eurydice and he holds her hand the entire way back…

Why is the dark so rich, so full of life? Why does he stare into it, lean into it? What is beautiful?

Erinýes draws Isaac to the island of Santorini. Isaac never confuses himself with Erinýes. She is the sharpest thing he'll ever touch. The room is red, with soft sunlight on the wood floor, and just now a breeze puffs up in the white curtains hanging at an open balcony door and hanging again at the open window.

Can he not desire to kill what is not himself?

This is where they live, in Santorini, a Greek island curved like a crescent moon in the Mediterranean Sea. Now it is nighttime; the sky that was aloof all day leans in. Erinýes loves Isaac but is not Isaac. Now, she imitates Polaris, and stands still inside of other circles, her periphery.

Erinýes walks toward the shore. It's late; the sky that was up in the rafters all day has dropped down an octave, and the cold, glassy store windows and doors now glow like bath candles. The air is smooth around her red nightgown, in her dark hair unbuttoned in the moonlight on her shoulders. She compares the stars to a crust of bread lying on the cobblestones beside a garbage can. Tonight, she is a mouse nibbling at the night, hungry for its largeness.

Why is the dark so rich?

If she tires of walking, then she lifts both feet and the sea slips toward her. She stops at a low stone wall that borders the white beach. She compares the stars to the sea. From this vantage, on the inside curve of the caldera, she can see the island homes that open up to the sea. The houses search, dark-eyed, the miles of curved beach.

Why is night so full of hunger?

The island cliffs slope down toward the sea, and she sees miles of white-faced, stone homes with bright blue trim in layers spaced out by stone staircases ascending to a road, descending to the sea. The island there resembles a falling wedding cake.

And here is the sea, cold on her foot, ankle, bone. The dark expands life. The dark is more interesting, in a sense fuller, maybe fuller with life. This is a strange reversal, since it seems that the clarity and definition that light gives should be what appeals to her, what she strives for.

She considers the construction of the caldera. A volcano is a bridge between worlds: inner and outer. Lava moves like a kind of message. It has the creative destruction of language, of a word. Lava is how she knows the earth's core, and the cold island is how she knows lava. Lava created the island. But there is more. Another prehistoric eruption shook the island, and the center collapsed, leaving only a curve of coastline. Now, there are three worlds, the inner, the outer, and the unseen. Also, there is light and dark and a red bedroom.

4. She replied, "That's what you think when you look in a mirror?"

"Can you close the door and sit down?"

She closes the door behind her, sits down in the driveway. Overhead, fast-swimming clouds reveal and obscure and reveal stars.

"Look at how fast those clouds are moving!" Isaac says.

"We're the ones moving."

"No, the clouds are moving. We are perfectly still."

"I wasn't talking to you. I was talking to the entire world."

5. She dreams the man of her dreams. (Forget everything I said
before.)

In the dark, without a knife to cut the way I must gently find
an open door, a handle that gives, the rusted hinge weeping.
What do we ever disclose? A cooling soliloquy. You are so
alone because you can never truly possess another. What can
tempt us with everything already taken away?

Your heart cave grows
stalactites and stalagmites.
I learn not to hurry
in the dark-throated passageways.
What can tempt me
with everything already taken away?

When I lie down, dreams tell me what I already know.
A large window is falling from my bedroom wall.
It dangles from one nail like an eye from its socket.
When it lodges, vertically, in the snow, the view
through it is snow fallen, still falling, late evening.

You are a cocoon now,
a dead memory I curl inside.
What wanted to be born here
inside your evacuated chambers?
How shall I excavate

How to Break Article Noun

without a bit of warmth or light?

My dreams confess my sins, but always too late:
how I left you cold, how I peered through glass at you.
The dreams are aware of my guilt, dig down in the snow,
it won't stay white for long. See? The opening to your cave,
a dead memory I curl inside. What wanted to be born here?

By now you have exhausted
every desire that composed you.
What has wings now? Here in
your old skin, what happened?
The truth remains in the hands
of the entombed saints.

6. He looks around, wonders for a moment, then remembers.

    A bright flame flaps along the horizon: an oil refinery. It's piercing, that light burning in the black sky. I look ahead: The road is licked smooth, gleaming beneath my headlights. The rain drops stop teetering out and now the whole cloud descends, expanding. The bare trees swim through vapors as I pass by. Elephantine limbs stretch out to fingertips, as must the subterranean tree parts, snaking into the earth for warmth. A branch opens up to light; a root descends down to nutrients. Both thirst. Which way? I am not lost. Mustn't each cell must choose its way? Mustn't each cell build a wall up into air or down into the world? A bridge over a lake. The glowing haze of a moon through clouds glints off the surface to strike my eye and, passing through the murky depths of the lake, perhaps strikes the eye of my reflected self. And then the question: who drives along the double of this road? His vehicle charging through the water, his hair rippling in the currents coming through the windows.

    There it is ahead, the glass hypothesis. The obsidian scales. The garnet eye. The steel skeleton.

7. Gleaming fish swim through my thoughts: Noelle is alone.

There's a girl here. She's been to the island for the weekend and is now back at this fancy hotel in Athens. She's sunburnt, but not badly, and anyway it's better than that washed-out color she usually is. Not that her fiancé minds her natural color; in fact he loves it. He loves everything about her. It's perfect. It's as if he had drawn a line around her to separate perfect from imperfect. There's hardly room for a word.

The sun shines sharply outside her window, casting acute angles along the gray bricks in the sill. She looks down to the small, optimistic garden, close to the building, surrounded by a chain snaking through a few iron posts. Over the trees, calm mountains mimic dark, upturned faces. She feels isolated in this sunny country, and absently wonders if he, the fiancé, is going to leave her. There's a little desk, and she sits down to write something. She thinks about leaving her little room and bites the end of her pen, but the invading day is so bright. She can't remember the last time it rained. She begins to imagine things.

In the lobby, she passes the concierge, whose round face swells in a smile.

The last time it rained, she was walking through Bratislava, looking for a menu in English or at least an internet café to send an email. She kept walking as a few drops became a light shower. The water trickled through the gray cobblestones under her red sneakers, toward the iron drains at the dips in the road.

It worsened. The already dim day darkened, and she paused under an awning beside a few other stranded pedestrians. A man with a long, brown beard leaned like a curtain against the wall by a door, his arms folded, watching the rain smack against the street. A pretty woman next to him in a pink suit and matching pink shoes read the Slovakian paper. Her eyebrows dipped while her pink lips pursed at something she was reading, and then she looked up at the weather. On the corner beside the woman, a man in a suit lit a cigarette and checked his watch.

She felt cold suddenly, though there was hardly any wind, and shivered. She stepped out into the remaining drizzle and plodded on. It was then that she realized her shoelace was untied and soaked, flipping around with each step, a gray fish out of water.

The doorman opens the door and she steps from the sharp, noontime shade of the hotel into the brilliant sunlight and sneezes. It's an embarrassing habit. Not that her fiancé minds it. She can feel the doorman watching her as she convulses forward, choo-chooing.

It had also rained before she left Louisiana. She'd been with him in his small cottage, the lights off, the sky gray through the open windows that let in the stormy air, the smell of fog. He was reading to her in the dim light. Beside him on the couch, she kicked her legs over his lap and leaned her head on his warm shoulder, and he paused to kiss her forehead. He'd been reading a French poem. She touched his neck and played with his soft hair. The language rolled on in his low voice. The hypnotic sounds rumbled through his chest. When she closed her eyes, she could forget everything except him. The rest of the world had collapsed, like a lung. It was like floating.

The sunlight pours over her. She watches her feet as she walks. A verse of a John Donne poem has wrapped around her mind. She listens to it as she walks. She hears it in his voice.

> For love all love of other sights controls,
> And makes one little room an everywhere.
> Let sea-discoverers to new worlds have gone,
> Let maps to other, worlds on worlds have shown;
> Let us possess one world, each hath one, and is one.

She can't tell whether she likes it or not. She wants to be a world, independent and vibrant. But her good habits have faltered. These days, she's asleep instead of awake every afternoon, sometimes watching cartoons when she can't sleep. She thinks about the fiancé too much, every time she looks someone else in the face, in fact. Her mom keeps telling her to just put the ring away. And these days, she just thinks about leaving her little room instead of really leaving it. By dinnertime, which is at 10PM in Athens, when her mom and some co-workers pick her up, she's not herself at all. She is ready to talk to really anyone.

She reaches the end of the hotel's marble driveway and turns left. She's in no hurry. It's hot, and she wants to pass through with as little exertion as possible. On the sidewalk, she is blanketed by melting heat shining from the sun and the hazy heat rising from the ground. She's already sweating through her shirt.

It also rained when they played miniature golf. They got to the 14th hole before it started. It had been an otherwise excellent day, cool for a Louisiana April because of the overcast sky. He liked overcast weather as much as she. The gray afternoon let out a soft rain; cool drops tingled on her bare arms. The turf soaked it in so that every putt kicked up a small wake around the ball. The air smelled like damp sod. She had sunk her first putt, and he wrapped her up in his wet arms, which felt immediately cool and warm, and swung her off her feet, her putter hesitating and tipping over.

Her feet are sweating against her sandals. In spite of the wearisome heat that squeezes her, she walks naturally. She'd do anything not to look like a tourist. She hates tourists.

She has forgotten that when her mom dragged her out to the Agora, she really had a great time climbing around on the low stone walls and broken columns of the old marketplace, the ancient ruins jagging up through the long weeds. She even liked hiking around with the tourists snapping pictures at the Parthenon.

The cobblestones are hard and broken. The sunlight is dazzling. Her shadow seems black and distinct, reflecting up at her like that.

She'd like to dream in that little room. But she thinks she sleeps too much. She'd like to write in that little room. But she says her mind wanders.

It rained on them in Philadelphia that May when they visited his hometown and parents. It didn't surprise them because, up north, the sky changes gradually. The air had become warm and moist, a sure sign, and the sky was a hazy, boggy gray. As they walked down 30th Street, she'd told him about Europe, about going away for a few months. Her mother had invited her along on a business trip. They had a two-for-one flight deal. They would share the corporate hotel room.

She was used to not understanding the things he said, but he said nothing, which was clearer than his words ever were. He shook his head as they walked, trying not to talk about Europe. It meant, *if you trusted me, then you'd belong to me.* Or worse, *we're in love and you don't exist without me.* She could see the demands he was making in his dark eyes. Silent demands. Plans for a perfect life. For a perfect other half. Perfectly absent. She felt the air thicken around her. She wanted to never go. She

116

wanted to go. She suddenly had nothing of her own. When the rain started, he took off running. They passed old, gray buildings crowding along the sidewalk, and some pedestrians huddled under shop awnings. They reached his car out of breath, the front car seats half-soaked beneath the slightly-open windows. He drove back, the car smelling like fog.

Her clothes stick and cling. In a clothing store window, a mannequin models a perfect size. Pretty, green trees grow out of small squares of dirt cut from the cobblestone sidewalks. Her arms swing. The sky is dazzling and bulging. The clouds drift slowly. The traffic is not loud but breezy. The air is light. The sun is bright as a bulb.

> For love all love of other sights controls,
> And makes one little room an everywhere.

If the man seems absent, then her hotel room must be nowhere and this street must be no place. She thinks she would like for him to be here, but then this no place would no longer exist. He says he would like to be here. He doesn't care how he cancels things out, places where they are not together, by holding everywhere in the palm of his hand like that. Or he does care, and he is busy canceling Athens out. Well, she knows that isn't right either. For him, there is simply a room that is an everywhere and that is all. His room.

How to Break Article Noun

There is no line at the subway station. She asks for two tickets by holding up two fingers. The man behind the counter is slumped like a pale, potted plant. He is sick of foreigners. He mutters quickly in Greek and she drops small change into the tray, unsure of the price. She's bought tickets before, but she forgets these things. He picks out the correct change and drops two small tickets with a nod. She smiles. He doesn't notice. She slides the change and tickets across the counter. The coins scrape with a hollow kind of ringing.

It rained at his family's timeshare on the Jersey shore. The light gray sky had met the dark water distantly. The wind had been strong and the sand had been soft and fine around her toes. The constant gusting had pushed his hair back from his perfect face. His eyes closed and he squeezed her hand. It was hard to breathe.

She reads on a pamphlet that when streetcars in Athens became public, they were drawn by mules. She imagines the clip-clop of two mules pulling the car as it lurches forward, their soft gray color. She holds a metal pole with three other passengers who are pressed together.

A young man boards, pulls a hand out of his jeans pocket to look at his watch. He's probably in college, she thinks. He reminds her of her little brother because of his dark eyes and freckles. She really wishes he would say something to her. Something in English. She again asks God silently what she's doing in Europe. The doors open. It's her stop. She steps through clustered people.

For love all love of other sights controls.

It becomes a song in her head. It warps and weaves steadily through itself to the beat of her steps. *All love of other sights controls. For love, all sights of other loves controls. For control, all sights of love all love of other. For love all love of love of other loves controls.* She knows that he's going to leave her. Walking now, she can feel the world, this country, this other room she's un-erasing. It's control that she wants back. He'll go on saying she hasn't loved him, she's lied to him all along, if she can just go away like this. She won't be sure he's wrong. She thinks that maybe love should erase all of her other sights, maybe real love forfeits control. She imagines love unmaking the world, two benevolent hands cracking the globe like an egg.

She pushes through the door of the internet café, whose name she can't, or at least doesn't, pronounce. The room is cool and dim, and the low music irritates her. The small tables are made of dark wood and the metal chairs are black. She checks the clock on the wall and sits down at a computer, the one she's used before. She opens up her email.

He hasn't written. It's only been a week since her last email, she tells herself. She has enough to say and begins a new email anyway. She likes to make things up, as a kind of exercise.

It is easy to say anything when you love me. Love makes

*a mess of me. I say so much that I come around to the beginning
again and have to start over. Nothing loves me like your silence.
I fill it over and over. The tide takes out every word. The silence
is freshly there to be written upon. I used to sleep there on the
salted sand. Now I run at it from far away. I run through forests,
valleys, mountains, to the edge of the sea. When I arrive, the
clean beach is too near. The erased words—there is no mention
of them. Not a scar on the flesh-colored sand. I understand how
the waters move. I have been their undulations. The only wound
is the solitude of this memory. I bury every word we have spoken,
but it is such a lonely task. There are none to help.*

    When your eyes beat down on me, whom do I see?

    *Your anonymous caresses are erased. The sea eats at the
shore and a precipice grows where the water has worn away the
beach. Sometimes I can feel my island shrinking. The air thickens
into a cloud. When I shiver, I feel you near. When I shiver, I feel
your embrace.*

    *But sir, I've begun to wonder, "What am I doing here?
Why should we be separate like this?"*

    *Of course, for all I know you've left me and you're
reading this from Houston. Maybe saying nothing is your way of
saying everything. Everyone agrees I shouldn't love you. And
still, we both know that you're already in Houston and I am as
alone as Athena herself. Well, goodbye.*

    She sends it and it's true. He has already left. She's
known it but couldn't bear it earlier, in her little room. There are
the letters she has sent, the unsent letters, the unwritten letters, the

letters she does not receive, and the invisible letters. Her hands sprawled on the keyboard remind her of someone else. A man at another computer has a putty face and is slumped forward in baggy, wrinkled clothes. A girl like a lime-green vase saunters into the café, surveys the customers, and exits. Goodbye, goodbye, goodbye, she thinks to herself like a spell. The computer hums warmly. The cursor blinks at her from the screen.

The phone rings, startling her. She leans across the desk to pick the phone out of its cradle.

"Hello?"

"Well hello, sleepyhead! Have you been cooped up in that room all day? Get outside!"

"It's raining outside, Mom!"

"Sweetheart, he called again. He's begging me for your number there. He says you're not answering any of his emails."

"He's exaggerating."

"Well, he asked me how you were, and I told him you're doing fine. You're doing fine, aren't you?" Her mom's voice drifts off, hesitantly. The girl doesn't want to talk about it, and ends the conversation.

The girl feels cold. She could get up to put on a sweater or change the temperature, but she's writing something in a notebook at a little desk. She'd rather be outside or talking with someone. She is tired of the small, good-smelling soaps in the bathrooms and the clean, white towels. She glances over her notebook at her reflection. She gets up to put on a jacket. She thinks she can feel her reflection, cool and steady in its frame, as she turns away.

She's been practicing not saying his name. She would like to erase him from herself. She thinks maybe he never existed, maybe she's made all of this up.

Now she's wishing she were hungry, because wanting food would be better than wanting absolutely nothing. She could take a bath or read some more, but she's clean and reading might put her to sleep, which she doesn't want. She looks at herself in the mirror again. Her complexion is much fairer than the Greek, and Athens' sun has really burnt her. Her forehead will peel soon, canceling her face, leaving a blank slate. She doesn't feel Greek or American or his by now. She thinks she's inside that verse of that poem, a citizen outside of his room that is an everywhere. Isn't it what she wanted? She fingers her ring nervously and feels like crying.

She thinks she used to matter. He is making her not matter. Past the gray brick windowsill, it's autumn. The distant mountains like upturned faces search the sand-colored sky, the dark clouds. An optimistic little garden huddles inside the blurry shadow of the five-star hotel. A lovely wrought iron fence snakes along its front. And there's her parents' mailbox with its tiny American flag. And there's those solid Louisiana clouds. She doesn't leave. It's perfect.

***

Carolyn Chun

VI: Motion & Emotion

1. He accidentally imagines her in pieces on his carving table.

I paint the outside of the door to the room containing you, the door through which we spoke. You paint the other side.

How to Break Article Noun

2. nothing (what am I except)

now there is nothing, less than nothing of
you, your hand ungrasps mine, your voice
thins to a thread, startles, and hesitates,
your dark eyes water and blank

and you vanish into a few inky marks on
this floor, every trace of you, your edges,
your hair and jaw and neck, every line
unhooks and sinks to this new

shadow of the way you whispered, the
way you _____when I leaned close
to your neck, I have dismantled your
breath, I've stripped every word

from the curve of my ear, I've unmade
you from me, feature by feature, your
ankle ungrasps mine, your skin thins to
a _____, startles, and hesitates, your

fingers murmur and blank, I've
sent back all of your belongings, and
until I am hollow of _____, in the middle
of the night, if my dreams remember

you I'll send those too

3. we will suppose them to be

On his way home one day, a man is for no reason distracted by a cloud, and passes by his usual exit in the wordless balance of his airy meditation. As he turns into the next exit, labeled "Silver Moon," he notices a glimmer out of the corner of his eye. He winces slightly at the light, and as the glimmer grows larger and brighter, he sees that it is the ocean. The man drives alongside it as the white beach stretches out, unoccupied.

The man considers it, the water and the sand, the glowing sun. A marvelous creation! Untouched by the violence of man. A suddenly-loud flatbed truck entering traffic discovers his little sedan too late to avoid him. The man swerves sharply out of his lane and steeply down into a ditch beside the beach, where his car comes to a halt at a precarious angle.

The man eases from his car and watches the truck howl away. Confident in the providence of the Almighty, he remains untouched by the encounter. His wife, too, shows no signs of alarm. She stands close to the man in the ditch, slightly below his feet.

The man has some mind to look at the beach, to observe the Almighty's perfect handiwork. He strolls toward the shore, his wife at his side. They remove their shoes when they reach the unadorned beach. As they walk across the sand, his wife disappears, her garments and hair being entirely sand-colored. The light is bright on the water and on the sand, and the couple has to proceed squinting into the light, so he doesn't notice the water until its cool touch. The man continues walking, and his wife appears again, sand-colored against the sparkling, blue-green water.

The man turns to look behind him, and sees the distant shore glazed with white foam, soft waves pushing one another toward the sand. The man looks down, and there he sees an expanse of ocean rippling under his feet. The man's expression surges with amazement and gratitude. He turns to his wife, his eyes blazing with joy and reflected light. At his sudden movement, her eyes flit in surprise to meet his. His full gaze startles her, and her mouth opens slightly as she backs up and away, from the surface of the water into the air. The man steps after her, clasps her hand, and kisses it, smiling radiantly. Where his hands and lips have touched her, an indigo-colored bruise blooms on her wrist and hand and spreads up her arm, stretching out along her skin. The same bruise spreads from the man's fingers toward his body. The couple rise without touching or moving again toward a blazing, white cloud in an otherwise empty sky. Their skins becomes darker and darker against the white of their untouched eyes. They float for a long while through the cloud over the ocean before they reach the skin of the atmosphere and ease gently through.

4. the contents of my life

A table with nothing but the bags of sugar. Seven bags.
The bags of sugar poured. The mound, the tiny spills descending.
The mound growing, the dust cloud rising. The mound, a nebula
in silhouette. The clean crystalline. The mound: O mound!
Unsullied shape! She reaches out: what if? what if? She pulls
back and delights.

A touch at last. One finger to the table, one granule
uplifted upon the fingertip. Her fingertip. One bit of mound. One
tiny mound uplifted. O mound! O mound upon the fingertip! O
mound upon the tongue! O mound dissolved into the blood!

His face regards her less than kindly. His monocle
pressed tight against the cornea for viewing. While she the mound
is tasting, he the mound is contemplating. Many granules, in the
pouring, rolled from the mound to the table. These she observed
as a penumbra of the brilliant mound. Her tongue is against the
table now—she can't resist, she captures the granules, each
distinct and glistening under close study. Noelle laps at the sugar,
pausing with the tongue outstretched. She raises her head up and
unplasters her tongue. Very delicately she takes it back into her
mouth. The granules dissolve, enter her blood. The Oh
concretion of delight! The Delight and augmentation, he corrects.
Oh Ah Ee Are you still here? she asks.

Delight and augmentation, Isaac says, over her shoulder.
Noelle turns, her hand upon her mouth, the tongue retreated.
What manner of greeting? she wonders. I give you sweet. I give

you cloud. I give you mound and spills descending, says he. What is sweet? What is give? What is cloud descending? she asks, but with her mouth covered it sounds like this: Wuh tuh swuh? Wuh tuh guh? Wuh tuh cluh duh mnd in? Her eyes swim.

You had forgotten me, he says. Don't talk that way! she demands, aquiver. You say all these ridiculous things, she says. You're so gnomic! she says. You, oh my dear, my dearest, clearest sundial, you are too much in the sugary sun, I'm the gnomon here to show you shadowy time, he says. Ahhhh! she says and yanks—what is it?—her hair!

His hair curls. Shh, he says. Shh. How could you forget? Deedle deedle do do ahhhh! she says, behind her hand. Isaac worries. O mound! he tries. O mound upon the fingertip! he tries. He climbs onto the table and sifts the sugar with his toes. He dips his knees into it. He covers and uncovers his mouth. O tiny mouth uplifted! he tries, touching her chin with a finger. O tiny mound uplifted! he tries, kicking up his sugar-soled feet.

Please please oh my love, the sugar, look, see the sugar, he says. Bbbbbbbbbbbbbbbb wokawoka bbbbbbbbb, he distinctly hears her respond. Please, look, he says, and stabs his finger into the very tiptop of the sugar mound, and presses it headstrong to the table with a Whoosh, the sugar erupting out into a crescent.

I am alone alone alone, she says. She looks away. She looks away. Isaac peers between his legs to see. The room is full of sugar cloud, the kicked up sugar mound. O dearest! O lovely! O perfect species! says he, offering her a sugar-clad toe. Her face has ossified. O darling! he says between his legs. This cloud, this haze: this heaven I've made. This angel I have made of you, he says. Now she is completely solid. He swims in sugar. This is how to swim! he says. Isaac presses his face into the flattened mound. He gathers it together again. Please, look, he says. O sugar crescent! he tries. Now she does not move. Now she does not creak and jaw. No, look, it's okay, look, he says, burying his face into the deep white caldera. He speaks with difficulty, sugar foaming on his lips, See, everything's okay, Mmm, sugar, mmm, good, see, mmm. Now she still is petrified, and he continues to roll himself in the sugar, gently cooing, gently cooing.

5. Isaac vs. Noelle. Am I the snow crunching or am I the boot?

"I hate you," Isaac says, looking up from his book. "You are as distant as my understanding of you presupposes."

Noelle wonders if he is reading out of the book. She recites the following lines from heart. "I don't hate those things about myself that you hate. I'm not there, but you're not here either."

Isaac looks back at his book. Again, he speaks. "You convinced me that you were here, but you're not. You wanted me to fight for a shadow and a dream of you. It was a lie and it was my only comfort in life. You could have been perfect."

"I don't want to fight," Noelle responds, unsure of her motives. She would like for him to leave. She would like for him to stay. Why doesn't he hold her? She is not too far away. Is she too far away? She tries to draw herself into the room. It hurts a little. "You belittled and hated me. You assaulted when I came near. What is left is distant. You were better off in Houston." Noelle wonders if she's crying now. She wishes she knew what she needed.

Isaac softens. He reads out of the book. "Here I'm just telling, to the best of my ability, the truth, to the best of my knowledge."

How to Break Article Noun

"That's no excuse. Why don't you say your heart is broken? Why don't you say what you don't know? Why don't you say the limits of your ability? Why don't you tell the truth better? Why don't you know more? Why can't you help us?"

Isaac holds the book up to block out Noelle's face. "You won't ever be wounded, that's how removed from us you are. It's a wonder I say anything to you. My genuine love and now hate are nothing to you. I was dull. Too charmed inspired by your childishness to see it clearly enough."

"You always hate me somewhere in there. Sometimes right on the surface. Why are we so injured by our differences?" Noelle begins to float off into this musing. She desires to be a letter written to him. A letter that he can read, as he is reading the book in his hands. He is right about her: She can't love him. She is a child. "You don't know what my joy is like or what my pain is like. I've wanted to live with you. Neither of us knows how. Now you rightly accuse me of cerebral, intellectual reactions to genuine love and hate. You rightly say that we can't mean anything to each other. The laws that govern us are immutable, as we now understand. There is no way for us to meet. There is no place for us to lie down." Her heart is breaking. Noelle wonders if it would be better to see herself as Isaac sees her.

"You don't even know me!"

"Who are you? Is this a real fight? Where is O

Susanna?"

Isaac sets the book down to look Noelle in the face. "Erinýes was right about you. You are a stupid little girl."

When she turns away, he presses his book too late against his open mouth. What has he done?

6. "Can you? Something???" Her. His. (It's all happened before.) He speaks.

Isaac opens the door at Noelle's hip bone and begins to climb her ribcage like a ladder. He sings as he goes, either aware of his song or unaware of his song.

> *In my dark space, you and a perfect loving.*
> *You know the words to still me.*
> *Words are no self, and are borne of not-knowing.*
> *They were born in a dark room.*

Her clavicle is the top rung of the ladder, and Isaac walks along it, arms outstretched, wobbling above her heart and lungs, toward the thick muscles of her neck, which resembles a tree trunk to him. It is not very dark inside her body, since the skin is lit by an exterior sun. Isaac grabs the muscle here and there and swings around to the cervical vertebrae, and begins to shimmy up the brainstem, still singing as he goes.

> *You I dream of loving, and dream of rooming.*
> *I love your dark roominess, in it I move, and dream of*
> *moving, and of being*
> *your words, and your eyes, and your body, and your dark*
> *rooms.*

Sidling into her skull, he laughs in the middle of his song.

Carolyn Chun

This laugh startles him—what's so funny? He enters the door in her lower left lobe, and clicks his heels together in the clean air. Isaac grasps the handle to the door to the visual cortex, pulls.

> *I die to give my self to you beyond all words. I don't have*
> > *it to give.*
> *Your self I cannot have or hold.*

The door swings open, and Isaac leans in. He rubs his eyes to make sure. The floor is a dark sponge, and through two floor-to-ceiling windows, Isaac perceives—himself!—his own constituents—his atoms splayed out like the stars of a galaxy.

> *Infinite as befits you, where you can dream happily,*
> *I am a perfect dark room with a dead man dreaming of*
> > *light.*

What is this emptiness? He lies down, now, his lips still forming words as he shivers in the dark theater, dwarfed by his own immensity.

> *You. You. Know the words. To drive me away.*
> *Perfectly perfectly perfectly perfectly—life is but a dream.*
> *You. I. Yearn to give. The incomplete world I contain.*
> *Your eyes and body are perfect, to me. Insane insane*
> > *insane.*

How to Break Article Noun

7. There are just enough clouds. She speaks.

I look up: how long have I been here?
The door is still closed, the night behind the small window
a blue reflection of a staircase and this room's light.
Whether I have been here for millennia or moments,
I look up; things are as they are.

I look up; is your face behind the door?
I don't know what to do; my heart knocks on its thin shell
knocks on the air I try to inhale and this room's light.
The walls come loose now, chunks of dry wall drop, and ceiling
        plaster.
I look at the ceiling, what color is it up there?

I look up at what is falling.
Bricks clap down on piles of bricks, the small windows
collapse, blue night fills in the holes: stars sky silhouette of tree
        fence far houses.
Next, the night swings over its hinges, revealing corners of a
        blank room.
I look up at what my heart is shaking loose.

I close my eyes: what are you doing here?
How have you followed me here (your eyes in all windows
are all windows) into black blank?
Lightning blazes neurons; thunder claps ventricles.

Carolyn Chun

I open my eyes: what are you doing here?

I touch you to encounter the world.
I touch you and encounter the world.

A day is composed of encounters:
I open out of your frame like a door.

A world is composed of molecules:
The molecules between your metacarpals.

Invisible electromagnetic forces of atomic matter:
Collide instead with a negatron. (The intersection is the world.)

Through high windows,
enter a larger room.

***

VII: Hollow

1. Something bad.

      She looks up at the closed door. His voice comes from miles away, "I want to do whatever you want me to do."

      "I have some work to do. I think I'll read a book, maybe this, maybe that—just leave. I think I please want you to just leave." The door is divided into seven panels. Not quite closed. Light from the hallway shines around the door's edges. It tilts open, casting a brief shadow on the wall of her face.

Carolyn Chun

2. Elementary opposites: dark clouds block out the stars.

What we have is a small remnant

of an utterly destroyed instrument.

I went outside but it was instead a small room.

I lit a candle and my shadow extinguished it: bloom

of an utterly destroying precision,

making and unmaking its own vision.

I lit a candle and my shadow unlit it: bloom

of a dying species, a smoking tomb

making and unmaking its own death.

Candle smoke swaying to the breath

of a dying species, a smoking womb.

I understood it I destroyed it I consumed it.

Candle smoke swaying to a tune.

I went outside but it was instead a small rune.

I understood it I destroyed it.

What we have is a small remnant.

3. pieces of volcanic glass

The night sky resembles the darkness of an open mouth. A great yawning mouth, its breath settling on her upturned face. He opens the car door.

She is still.

The moon has set or else not yet risen. Isaac isn't sure. It's late, and the words aren't there: he doesn't know what to say. He has something to say, but he doesn't know what. It doesn't matter now, though. He says nothing and turns the key in the ignition.

She is still lying on the red couch. Either she is asleep or she is awake. If she is asleep, then either she dreams or she does not dream. If she dreams, then either she is the hero or the villain of her dream. If she is the hero, then either she swallows the earth or she is swallowed whole by the earth, a shift in the earth's mantle, then another shiver, and a third bringing a bloody chasm beneath her feet, the chasm descending into his throat. If she swallows the earth, then either another world grows in her belly, or every light remains extinguished. If another world grows in her belly, then either she will weep to fill the dry oceans or the world will remain a tomb.

Isaac drives, the failed world falling behind him. He

desires something he cannot say. Unarticulated, it rests in the moving car. Perhaps dormant. Perhaps eclipsed: has he cast his shadow on it? Where is the moon? Invisible, inchoate. Forfeited, forfeited. The unadorned moon. The naked moon somewhere hidden in his shadow is the only thing he longs to touch. As he drives, the trees shrouding the road finally part to reveal the dark sky, which absorbs him. The trees, unnoticed by him, move away in lines toward opposite horizons. The moon has set or else not yet risen.

The world is the only thing large enough. The world is not large enough. If she weeps the seas, then she may flood the earth. If she leaves, then she may pass through the visible and invisible galaxies, the unseen untold, the unknown emptiness, where nothing is able to live. If she lives on Neptune, then she may fashions Triton with her tears, a moon to revolve in retrograde, hoping that this moon will untie her from her own orbit. If so, then either she will fail to be released or she will succeed.

Isaac pauses by an empty field beneath the sky. He stops the car, closes the door behind him. Snow crystals land on the car windshield and in his hands. The stars and planets glow above him. His breath condenses: the air fills with fog, silhouettes of fish flip at the edges.

Triton is a cold moon. Triton cannot relieve her.

"When you look at me a light within me expands to touch all the points of the visible universe."

4. "Can you close… and sit…? Don't you love me enough?" he
said. He hasn't yet…

the shadow of a door is a door the
reflection of a door is a door the
light shining around the edges
of a door is a door and the memory
of a door is also a door

5. The white blanket kicks in response. *Don't you love me enough?*

aloNe I scale

Sometimes my mind calls your name.
Sometimes I hear your voice call back.
I never say your name out loud,
nor do you answer.

Your name is just a word like any other
word that may be spoken. Write down
words. Erase them. Words can be cleaned
like anything else. Time takes you letter by letter.

I hope that you enjoyed the spaces that we made.
Sometimes our names fit together into new words.
Erasing your name leaves mine, just jumbled up.
Our bodies made spaces. Our minds made spaces.

The space between two bodies can contain cosmic
distances or moons. Gravity will or will not hold
things together. When I loved you, my fingers touched
infinite skies we inhabited: clean space, pure space.

I hope that you enjoyed the contours of my mind.
Sometimes our names fit together into new words.

Carolyn Chun

I could lie down in that created space,
my fingers brushing the sparking clouds.

Words could not travel the miles between us.
I never say your name out loud.
Sometimes I hear your voice call back.
Sometimes my name calls your name.

6. He glides through

Hic.

"Scientists have proven conclusively, Isaac, that humans have nothing whatsoever to say to one another. In light of this evidence, I suggest we, that is, oughtn't we, you know, et cetera et cetera?"

Noelle is shivering. Her arms are bare. Isaac is bundled in a coat and scarf. A pile of curly brown hair, a pale forehead, dark eyes that look away, nose, scarf. She wonders why he's walking down this hallway. She's sure it's him, and wonders that she doesn't feel a thing now, looking at him, shivering. It's been years. An eternity.

Ille.

Years ago, in winter, at night, a garden. He pulled open a door. She stepped in. The air expanded in the bright conservatory. The immense room bloomed, a marble path cut through the carpet of flowers, shrubs, and trees, enclosing the rectangular garden center. Flowering vines covered hanging cauldrons; rows of poinsettias lined the front of the garden; white Rhaphiolepis trees here and there. The conservatory was warm, and Noelle unwrapped her scarf and coat. The scent, the moist air, the green white and red. From somewhere, the sound of water.

Along the paths, labeled flowerbeds, shrubs, and trees.

Oleander (*Nerium oleander*). Crape-myrtle (*Lagerstroemia indica*). Golden lily (*lilium auratum*). Calla lily (*Zantedeschia*). Daffodil (*Narcissus jonquilla*).

"The sound of water is actually, I've been meaning to tell you, the sounds of bubbles popping in the water. The size and depth of the bubbles, as well as the speed and temperature of the water, there's lots to factor in, that is, et cetera."

The room's interior exceeded the volume of the surrounding cold air night universe. The Red Stem Dogwoods, the roses and primroses, the winter hollies, the aquarium of orchids. In the center of the garden, a flat slab of marble shining beneath a thin layer of water, reflecting the countless blossoms. At the center of the marble slab, an emerald bouquet of ferns.

Hic.

Isaac pauses in the hallway. Noelle strangely feels nothing, shivering. He stoops over a water fountain. She could say, "Water is the only compound that exists naturally in solid, liquid, and gaseous forms on earth's surface. Because water becomes less dense upon freezing, unlike any other substance, life is able to exist on this planet. If ice sank, then frozen ponds would be unable to melt. This planet would be frozen and dead. It would have never lived. Usually, you see, molecules become closer when they freeze. Tighter. Denser. But water is densest when it is in liquid form. The molecules space out when the water freezes into a solid. There's a space."

Ille.

       Isaac and Noelle looked at each other. He extended his right hand and, at the same time, she her left. Hand in hand, they climbed through euphorbias, through cyclamens and begonias, through Amaryllis, to the marble slab. Isaac and Noelle crouched at the water's edge. Isaac touched the surface with his index finger, and then pressed down with his whole hand. The water held the impression of his hand, froze beneath his touch, solidified and blanched opaque. The freeze spread over the marble slab in a ripple. Isaac and Noelle rose to their feet and stepped onto the ice.

       "The moon's ice caps contain a mixture of water and *regolith*, or moon dust. The presence of water on the moon permits the possibility for the moon to sustain life. Some other planets' moons have water in the form of ice, for example Neptune's moon Triton. The biochemical reactions needed to sustain life require a medium such as water to occur. Water is able to dissolve more compounds than any other liquid. Water bends enzymes. It is a naturally occurring inorganic liquid. The sound of water is the sound of life as we know it, et cetera, ad infinitum."

       Isaac stepped gingerly across the white ice. Noelle beside him held his arm. She looked up at his red cheeks, the misty puff of breath at his lips. They moved by slipping and regaining their balance in a process that did not resemble walking. At the planter in the center, they stopped.

Hic.

"There is somebody in this hallway," she could say. Or, "Why here? Why not in other corridors at other times? We dissolved and drew near and passed through each other. Things solidified between us cold distant quiet." But she does not say any of these things. He is past her now, and almost to the door. She strangely doesn't feel a thing. She shivers. Her face feels cold, and her feet are frozen to the floor.

Ille.

Isaac touched the bright green fern. From beneath his finger, a wave of frost spread across the surface of the fern, labeled "Emerald Queen." (*Nephrolepis obliterata*). The lights extinguished in the conservatory.

7. sinks back down from the rafters as the temperature goes out of the house.

       She looks up at the closed door. His voice comes from miles away, "I want to do whatever you want me to do."
       "I have some work to do. I think I'll read a book, maybe this, maybe that—just leave. I think I please want you to just leave." The door is divided into seven panels. Even so tightly closed, light from the hallway shines around the door's edges. It tilts open (he's pressed the handle) casting a brief shadow on the wall of her face. Her mouth flutters open and shut without a sound. It would be too easy to make him sorry.

***

Carolyn Chun

Vita

Carolyn Chun was born on November 30, 1980 in Pennsylvania. She attended Rutgers University from 1998 to 2002, where she majored in mathematics and physics. Carolyn spent the next year tutoring traveling and visiting family. In 2003, she moved to Baton Rouge, Louisiana to study mathematics. Carolyn received a doctor of philosophy in mathematics and master of fine arts in creative writing from Louisiana State University, both awarded in August, 2009. She is currently a postdoc in the school of mathematics, operations research and statistics at Victoria University in Wellington, New Zealand, and is supported by a grant from the National Science Foundation.

Printed in Great Britain
by Amazon